MCKENZIE RAE

My Dark Passenger

To my mom, who shares my love of dark stories.
And to Karina, because she told me to.

Contents

Acknowledgments

This book has been through a lot. My goal was to finish writing it during the month of October, which I managed to do. After that, I didn't know what to do with it. I considered making it my first self-published book but chickened out. Then I discovered Crazy Ink Publishing, and Erin Lee decided to take a chance on me. *My Dark Passenger*, and the books that follow it, may have remained in my Google Drive indefinitely if it hadn't been for her and the amazing team at Crazy Ink. Although this book is no longer published with them, it would not be where it is today without Erin and every one of the talented, generous people who worked with her.

This book was also made possible by my parents, who have always believed in my dream to become an author and encouraged and supported it. One last shout out to my best friend and honorary sister, Karina, who has made my writing better without crushing my sensitive writer's heart.

1

Thou Little Tiny Child

Imagine walking through a forest and coming to a fork in the overgrown dirt road, with crunchy, autumn-colored leaves cushioning your feet. That's from a Robert Frost poem, isn't it? I'm not a poetic guy; I haven't read or written poetry since my college days, but this poem sometimes comes to mind.

We don't truly see those forks in the road of life until years later. In theory, we're all aware that our decisions have consequences, and by choosing one option over another, the second option is left unexplored. But we don't truly understand all of the opportunities we missed until we're older.

Sometimes, it's the job we didn't take. It's the man or woman we let walk away. For some of us, it's the times we didn't say, "I love you." If we had just said it one more time, would anything have been different?

There are many decisions in my life that I think about and ask myself, "What if?" One memory in particular that I always come back to is this.

It's the gas station just off the highway. I saw the sign for it as I passed the exit ramp. I remember glancing down at the needle on the gas gauge and thinking that I would be fine. I could make it to the next gas station.

Except there wasn't another gas station.

If I had stopped at that gas station when I saw the sign, then maybe this whole thing would have been avoided. I never would have met you. Sometimes, I wonder if that makes you sad—the idea of never meeting me. I wonder if you feel anything at all.

The guy who wrote that poem said that he took the road less traveled and that it had made all the difference. Every time I hear that bit quoted, it's always spun as something positive and hopeful. Does the poem ever say that, though? That his life is happy, meaningful, and fulfilling? He just says that it made all the difference. That could mean anything, couldn't it?

I also took a road that few, if any others, traveled, but I didn't go alone. I let you jump into the passenger seat of my truck.

I wouldn't be where I am today without you.

* * *

Trees in vibrant shades of green, brown, red, and orange are painted in grays and blacks at night. The clear, dark sky bathes the highway and surrounding forest in silver moonlight. Rural roads possess a stark beauty, accompanied by the sounds of crickets, owls, and bats. Despite the breathtaking sights, I don't want to park on the shoulder of the highway tonight and sleep in my truck.

Where did all the gas stations go? Did I drive off the edge of the map? There's no way the tank should be empty before I see another sign for fuel. And of course, cell service out here is nonexistent. I'm more likely to find a pot of gold at the end of a rainbow than to get AAA on the line.

Heaving a weary sigh, I get out of the truck and slam the door. I don't know much about cars, but I've gotten to know my own vehicle fairly well over the years. It's a blue Chevy, and I know I have fifteen miles to empty once the idiot light comes on.

I stuff my hands in my pockets to keep them warm and start walking. The weather could be worse, I concede, trying to find a silver lining. At least it's not raining or snowing. If I didn't have the moon to light my way, I'd be screwed. The flashlight I keep in my emergency kit hasn't worked in ages. I keep saying I'm going to replace it, but that's a problem for future me.

A choir of crickets chirps in surround sound. Every now and then, I see the silhouette of a bat flit overhead, squeaking to its friends. The hooting owl sounds much farther away. It's probably not the safest thing for me to be doing, walking down a lonely highway in the dead of night without reflective gear. If my mom could see me now, she'd have a fit.

Two-thirds of a mile from my useless truck, I see the well-lit sign for a BP station. It kills me a little knowing how close I was. There's a big semi in the parking lot, but nobody else is around except for two employees working the night shift. One is a younger guy in his early twenties. The other is a middle-aged woman, not much older than me.

The kid mops the floor while the woman flips through a People magazine. They spare me a glance when I walk through the door before going back to their respective tasks. I grab a flashlight and a pack of batteries, and then I go up to the counter to pay for them and a gas can. The woman reluctantly sets aside her magazine and appraises me as she rings up my card.

"Long night?" she asks in a heavy smoker's voice.

"Yeah," I answer, followed by a yawn.

"Same," she mutters. "There's a Super 8 just down the road if you're looking for a place to stop."

"Gotta go back for my ride first." I take my card from her and stuff my wallet into my back pocket. "Thanks, though."

I've got the gas can in one hand and my new flashlight, batteries loaded, in the other when I head outside. Under the white lights bathing the parking lot, I pause. Something feels off. It's not the chorus of chirping crickets still singing just as loudly or the breeze that's just as cool as it was earlier. It's not the stars that shine just as bright. I can't pinpoint what it is, but I can feel it. A shift in the atmosphere.

After I cross the street and get away from the station lights, I turn on the flashlight. The circular beam goes ahead of me down the slope of the exit ramp. Those shades of gray and black are temporarily interrupted by the light. Then the beam sweeps in the opposite direction, and the night swallows those colors whole.

Anxiety undulates under my skin as I hike back to my truck. It's funny how I'm more anxious now that my path is lit than I was when I made this same trip in the dark.

A sound to the left makes me freeze. The beam of light swings across the ditch and hits the line of trees. Only tendrils of light sneak past the rough trunks and spindly branches. I think the flashlight actually makes it harder to see if anything or anyone is out there. The light is just creating more shadows.

When I don't hear anything else, I start moving again. Gravel crunches under my shoes. I stare at my feet for most of the walk. There's a sense of exposure out here. I fight the urge to make myself smaller and hide. It feels like someone is watching me, hidden among the color-eating shadows. If anything is nearby, it's probably a deer, scared spitless and trying not to be noticed by me.

Regardless, I can't shake the mounting fear rising in the center of my chest. It pulsates with each breath, each heartbeat, each footstep.

I see my truck from a long way off. The highway is flat and straight, so it's easy for the beam to catch the reflective glass of the headlights. As I hurry to it, I start to breathe a little easier. By the time I make it to my destination, the irrational fear has dissipated. Unscrewing the gas cap, I chuckle at myself. What the hell's the matter with me?

Just in case the perceived danger wasn't completely a figment of my imagination, I let the light roam all around the vehicle. There's nothing. Nobody is here—no animals either. I'm about to open the driver's door when I pause.

I don't know why. The fear hasn't returned; it's something else. Like when someone is staring at me from across the room, and I can somehow feel their gaze on the nape of my neck. Impulsively, I lift the flashlight and shine it through the window. On the other side of the truck, staring back at me, is a pale face.

My pulse spikes, and a shiver raises the hairs on my arms.

It's a girl's face, round like a full moon and framed by two curtains of dark hair. Eyes that are just as dark study my face intently. Her expression is blank. I have no idea how she came to be watching me through the passenger window since I walked around the perimeter of the truck minutes ago and didn't see her. Keeping the light pointed in her direction, I start to edge around the hood.

"Can I help you?" I ask cautiously.

She doesn't respond. Maybe she's scared. At nearly six feet tall, I'm not exactly a small guy, and from the position of her face in the window, I can tell she can't be many inches over five feet herself.

She's a petite little thing, I see as I come to face her head-on. The features of her face are delicate: a button nose and a pouty mouth. Now that I'm not looking at her through two windows, I notice her black hair is dyed. The roots are a lighter brown. Her arms hang by her sides, ending in thin wrists and dainty fingers. Her legs give her a bird-ish appearance, with knobby knees and tapered ankles. She's wearing some kind of uniform, like those used at private schools. A long sweater, pleated skirt, and clunky black shoes.

She stares at me and doesn't say a word.

"Are you in trouble?" I venture, unsure why a young girl would be on the side of a highway in the middle of the night. She can't be any older than fifteen or sixteen.

The girl doesn't answer me. Doesn't even shake or nod her head. Just continues to stare.

It isn't like she's in a trance. She sees me; I can tell. It's more like she can't hear me or doesn't understand, but she doesn't seem to care what I'm saying anyway.

"Are you deaf?" I ask, although I don't know sign language.

Again, she doesn't respond. She doesn't look confused or concerned, giving me zero indication if she hears me. Maybe she speaks a different language. She doesn't look Latina, but I guess she could be. I only know a handful of words in Spanish from high school and a tiny bit of Swedish that Grandma taught me when I was a kid.

While I'm debating how to try to communicate next, the girl finally averts her eyes. She looks over my truck, running her fingers along the paint, which is rusted and flaking in some places. Her fingers curl around the door handle. She pokes at the keyhole and tilts her head.

I clear my throat. "Listen, if you need a ride somewhere, I can take you. But you gotta talk to me."

She pulls on the handle experimentally and stumbles when the door opens.

Without hesitation, the girl climbs into the passenger seat of my truck. She doesn't close the door; she just sits there with her hands resting in her lap. When I move closer, she doesn't flinch or eye me warily. Not the way most teenage girls would behave when faced with a strange man.

The girl looks at me again when I extend my hand to her.

"I'm Kevin Wolf," I say. "Most people just call me Wolf."

Her gaze drops to my hand. It's impossible to guess what she's thinking. After a minute, the girl raises one hand and slips it into mine. I grasp it gently. She doesn't squeeze or even grip my hand. Her fingers sit limp against my own.

The girl's skin is cool. Not cold, not hot. It's smooth, too. I feel the softness over the ridge of every knuckle.

"What's your name?" I ask.

Silence.

I release her hand, which she returns to her lap.

"So, you need a lift?" I ask, receiving no response. "Well, let's at least get you off the highway," I suggest, shutting the door.

As I go to get behind the wheel, I hesitate. There's that feeling again—not the fearful one, but more like what I first felt when I left the gas station. A shift in the air.

I turn the key in the ignition and listen to the engine growl.

"Where are you headed?" I ask, though I realize she won't answer. "I'm going northwest," I inform her.

She tilts her head and looks at me. Her demeanor is like the surface of a lake on a windless day—calm and undisturbed. Except that there are no fish in this lake. No insects, turtles, ducks, loons, or boats disturb the water, which lies flat like glass.

I have enough gas to get to Sycamore tonight. In the morning, I can hand her over to the cops and let them handle Little Miss Silent.

* * *

Carson is the only guy I've ever met who can genuinely rock a mullet. He's also the only cop I know—at least, the only one I know on good terms. It's been a year since I last saw him, but I still know where to find him on a weekday morning. I pull into the parking lot of the only Perkins for miles around. After engaging the parking brake, I look at the girl beside me.

We drove through the night. She didn't speak or sleep, and despite this, she doesn't appear tired. Personally, I'm exhausted. The only thing on my mind is a strong cup of coffee. The girl looks at me through the curtain of her unwashed hair.

"You want breakfast?"

No answer. I'm too tired for this.

"Okay." I crank down my window. "We've got an open window, and I'm leaving the doors unlocked. If you need more air, step outside. If you get hungry, come in and find me. I need to talk to an old friend, but it shouldn't take long."

This Perkins in Sycamore is one of those places I associate with very specific memories. A sense of nostalgia envelops me when I catch sight of Carson. I nod to the hostess and walk to his table, claiming the seat across from him. He looks the same as ever, shirt sleeves rolled up to show off his tattoo sleeves, brown hair touching his shoulders in the back, short and messy up front. He smiles as soon as he sees me.

"You order anything for me, Carson?"

"Wolf! Woof, woof, woof!" he hollers like he always does when we meet. I grab his coffee and gulp down what's left. Wincing, I force myself to swallow.

"That is battery acid," I croak. "I don't understand the appeal of black coffee."

"I'll get teased mercilessly if anyone around here catches me ordering a drink with some ridiculous name," he replies. "I don't know anyone who actually likes black coffee." Carson flags down the server and asks for another cup. "I haven't seen you in months, Wolf. That time of year already?"

I grunt and nod.

The server delivers a second cup and fills it to the brim. I mumble thanks and proceed to dump two creamers and four packets of sugar into the dark drink. Carson waits until we're alone before diving back into conversation.

"So, how've you been?"

"Have you had any kids go missing around here recently?" I ask, ignoring the pleasantry.

"Well, I'm doing good, Wolf. And yourself?" Carson raises an eyebrow expectantly.

I roll my eyes. "How're you doin', Carson? How're the wife and kids?"

Carson beams. "Still nonexistent, but thanks for asking. See, that wasn't so hard. Polite conversation is the only thing separating us from the animals." I nod throughout his spiel. It's the same thing every time we see each other. I try to skip the small talk, and he insists on it. "Now, what's this about a missing kid?"

I rest my elbows on the table. "Have you heard of any missing girls about fifteen or sixteen years old?"

Carson leans back in his chair, eyes drifting upward thoughtfully. "Recently, huh? We had a runaway back in April, but that was a thirteen-year-old boy. He got as far as Foley before someone recognized him and called it in. But a girl … I can't think of anybody since Aileen Swanson disappeared. Except that was thirty years ago, and she was never found. Why?"

I tell him about the girl in my truck and explain how she came to be there. My story ends in the Perkins parking lot.

"You left her in the truck?!"

"I rolled the window down and left the doors unlocked," I say defensively. "What was I supposed to do? She didn't want to come in. Should I have thrown her over my shoulder and carried her inside?"

"No, but you could have mentioned that there was a kid waiting alone in your truck."

Carson gets up, grabs his uniform jacket, and fishes some cash out of his wallet for a tip.

"I tried telling you as soon as I got here, but we had to go through all the how-do-you-dos first. Polite conversation is the only thing separating us from the animals, Carson."

"Yeah, yeah. Let me pay, and then I'll meet you outside."

The door gently swings closed behind me. A crisp breeze has picked up since I've been in the restaurant, carrying the sweet scent of dead leaves.

I jog across the parking lot. Soon, this whole thing will be over, and I can be on my way. I'll hand the girl over to Carson, and he'll make sure she gets back to her family.

Coming up to her window, I raise my fist, prepared to rap my knuckles on the glass. That doesn't happen, though. The passenger seat is empty. So is the driver's seat. I peer through the narrow window in the back, but she hasn't climbed into the rear of the truck either. Spinning on my heels, I scan the parking lot. Carson is coming out of the Perkins and making a beeline for me. I look up and down rows of cars, hoping to spot her but having no luck.

"Hey." Carson's cheeks are reddened by the breeze as he stops beside me. "Where's the girl?"

I shake my head. "I swear, she was just here."

"She's not in the truck anymore?"

Carson goes through the same motions I did, even looking underneath the vehicle. Then he helps me comb the rest of the parking lot, thinking maybe she just stepped out to stretch her legs. The parking lot is empty of people. There's no trace of her.

Carson gives me a look. It's a look he hasn't given me in seven years, like he's worried about me, like I might do something stupid.

"Wolf," he approaches me cautiously, "how many hours have you been driving?"

I rub a hand over my face. "I'm not hallucinating, okay. I will put my hand on a Bible!"

"Hey, I believe you. I'm just saying I don't think you should go anywhere until you get a nap in." He takes his phone from his pocket. "Tell me what she looks like again. I'll check our database. See if anyone matches her description."

He doesn't believe me. He believes that I believe it, but he thinks I'm exhausted. I am, but not to the point of seeing things. I reiterate the description I gave him over coffee. Then he says he has to get to work and suggests I sleep in the truck for a while. He only leaves after I agree.

Once he's gone, I take another look through the parking lot. I know I won't find anything, but I feel a kick in my chest. The one that I feel whenever I know I'm right. I shouldn't be so determined to find the girl. I don't want her. I didn't even order breakfast; that's how eager I was to get her out of my hair. So why am I searching for her now that she's gone?

Whatever, it doesn't matter. Peeved and tired beyond belief, I yank open the driver's door and push the seat down as far as it will go. It's not the most comfortable position to sleep in, but it will do. The second that my body is semi-horizontal, I'm dead to the world.

* * *

It's night once more, and I'm back in the truck. I stare out the window, watching the headlights illuminate the blur of trees rushing past. It's silent except for the rumble of the engine. The white noise is comforting, though mostly drowned out by the suffocating darkness pressing in around me. The night closes in and reaches for me. I need something to hold it at bay.

I reach for the stereo and twist the dial. Nothing happens. Not even static comes through. Is it broken? I switch dials, trying to tune it to a different station. Still nothing: no static, no music, no late-night programs. I can't see any damage to the stereo; nothing indicates that something is wrong. Leaning back in my seat, I fold my hands in my lap and wonder what I'm going to listen to to keep myself awake.

Then it hits me. My hands are clasped together, and there is no steering wheel in front of me. If I'm not driving, then who is?

The thought of turning my head paralyzes me. I have a childish notion that if I can't see the driver, then they can't see me. Or maybe it's more like if I pretend to be ignorant of their presence beside me, then I'll be safe. Whatever the reason, trying to move my neck makes me sweat and shiver. I can only bring myself to look at the driver's seat from the corner of my eye.

A black silhouette hunches over the wheel, a hood drawn over their head. Slowly, the figure starts to turn in my direction.

With a startled jerk, I wake up.

I'm still in the Perkins parking lot. My spine and shoulders ache from the awkward sleeping position in the truck. I reach for the lever to raise the back of my chair when something catches my eye in the passenger window.

The pale face of the girl stares at me, and I swear under my breath. Reaching across the seat for the handle, I push the door open.

"Where were you?" I demand. "I wasn't inside for ten minutes, and when I came out, you were gone!"

I can't figure out why anger swells in my chest. I don't know this girl, so I shouldn't care. As before, she says nothing. However, this time she points to a car parked several spaces away from the truck. My mouth twists into a frown. It seems Carson had the right idea; our search just wasn't thorough enough. I scowl at her.

"You were hiding under a car?"

Rubbing the sleep out of my eyes, I press knuckles into my eyeballs until stars appear. Finally, I resurface and gesture toward the passenger seat.

"Get in."

Without a sound, she obeys. It doesn't cross my mind to take her to the police station until much later. Maybe because she hid from Carson, and subconsciously I realized that's not what she wanted. But I'm not that intuitive, so I don't think that's the case. The reason doesn't matter. The point is, I don't drive to the police station to drop her off. I pull out of the parking lot and drive down the road with my silent passenger in tow.

2

Kissed the Girls and Made Them Cry

I still have that dream sometimes: the one where someone else is driving my truck. It's always in the middle of the night, and the driver is just a black shadow. I can't quite explain why it scares me the way it does.

I've often wondered why you chose me. Yes, I was probably the only person to run out of gas on that particular highway that night. But after that, why me? Why didn't you go with Carson? Or hitch another ride from someone else when I left you in the truck at Perkins? There was a busy road right there; surely someone would have picked you up. I used to question why I didn't take you to the police station after waking up from my nap and seeing you were back. That's what I _should_ have done.

But I don't wonder about that anymore. I've come to accept there was something about you—something that made people do things they wouldn't normally do.

Were we headed to the same place? Did the destination even matter? I have so many questions now that you're gone, questions I never thought to ask. I'm torn between wanting you to return for just five minutes so I can get some answers, and praying fervently that I never see you again.

I used to feel guilty for praying like that. Not just praying to never see you again, but praying that wherever you were, you were dead. I thought I was a terrible person because you were just a girl. For all I knew, you were innocent. But now, I believe you knew something bad would happen if you stayed with me. You just didn't care.

* * *

We drive out of Sycamore in silence, which has become expected. Under different circumstances, I'd spend the day here, hanging out with Carson when he's free. Today, I make a quick stop at the gas station to fill the tank and buy food. It doesn't cross my mind to say goodbye to him before leaving town. It only occurs to me twenty miles away that maybe I should have.

For breakfast, I've had three donuts and gulped down a cup of gas station coffee. There are still plenty of donuts left in the box after I take my share. I picked a variety since I'm not sure what she likes to eat. But who doesn't like donuts, right? There's powdered, glazed, chocolate, jelly-filled, and cream-filled. I also grabbed a few juice bottles: apple, orange, and grape. Surely, she'll like one of those.

So far, the girl hasn't touched anything. With one hand on the wheel, I open the box between us.

"Want one?" I ask, my mouth half full of pastry. She looks from me to the donuts.

"Come on," I tease with a smile. "You better eat at least one, or I'll end up eating them all. And that won't be good for either of us."

She stares at the donuts for a while before finally picking a jelly-filled one. She doesn't eat it right away; she just holds it. It's a small gesture, but it gives me hope. By now, I've concluded something's wrong with her—whether she's mentally disabled or traumatized. Either way, accepting food feels like progress. And she did try to communicate with me back in the Perkins parking lot!

Encouraged, I point to the plastic bag at her feet. "If you're thirsty, I've got apple juice, orange juice, and grape juice. Take whichever you like."

Holding the donut in one hand, she leans over and rummages through the bag. She carefully inspects each bottle before selecting the apple juice.

Now in daylight, I notice her attire again. What I thought was a private school uniform lacks any school crest—it's just a plain gray sweater with a white shirt collar peeking out. She's not wearing socks or stockings, just clunky black shoes. Scratches and bruises mark her pale legs, covered with a fine dusting of black hair that's grown out. It seems like she hasn't shaved in several days. Though I find the weather pleasant enough, I'm dressed in jeans and a jacket. She must be cold in that skirt.

I turn the heat up higher than usual. "Let me know if it gets too hot for you."

I doubt she will, so I'll have to keep watch. I briefly consider offering her something of mine to wear, but everything in my bag would be too big. If I come across a convenience store with clothing, I'll buy her a pair of sweatpants.

I turn on the radio and flip from commercial to commercial to bad country music. I stop on NPR, which tends to be boring, but it's a different kind of boring than advertisements. It's not mindless, and sometimes they discuss a topic that captures my attention—although not today. I've been so out of touch with current events that I can't make heads or tails of what this program is discussing. It sounds political.

I glance at the girl. She appears neither interested nor bored, simply staring out the window at the trees flying by.

It takes a while, but eventually, I kind of forget she's present. Gradually, I zone out and drive on autopilot while vaguely listening to the soothing voices on the radio. Without interruptions, I can turn my truck into a time machine, driving into the past until I'm ten years younger, heading up north with a passenger who is generally pretty chatty, except when she falls asleep with her temple pressed against the window. We're going to visit my parents in the small town of Birchwood Lake. Every year, the town hosts its Fall Festival. We'll buy caramel apples and go to the pumpkin patch.

I am able to live inside my time capsule until noon, when my stomach growls. The donuts are gone, even the one the girl chose. The residue of red jelly has dried on her fingers. It's funny, I think. I never noticed her eat it. The apple juice bottle is empty too.

I pull off the highway and drive toward a gas station and McDonald's that share a building. A bell rings overhead when the girl and I walk inside. This gas station has a larger convenience store than most, and I quickly spot two round clothing racks. There's also a shelf lined with T-shirts. We must be near a college town since everything is emblazoned with a university label and is unabashedly overpriced.

Feeling a presence at my side, I glance down. The girl stands a hair's breadth from my elbow. In my periphery, I notice the lady at the register giving me the stink eye. Yeah, I know how it looks. I'm a guy in his late thirties, alone with a teenage girl who looks slightly shell-shocked and is dressed like a Catholic schoolgirl. I put a little distance between the girl and me and grab the first article of clothing I touch. Her shoes squeak on the linoleum as she follows me to the counter.

While I pay, the woman at the register casts meaningful looks at the girl. What she is attempting to silently communicate is either lost on the girl or she's being purposefully obtuse.

Once my wallet is a little lighter, I tear the tags off the clothes and thrust them into the girl's skinny arms. "Here's something clean you can wear until we wash the clothes you've got on," I say, pointing to the sign above the doorway. "Restrooms are that way."

I pray she doesn't need help dressing herself. Despite appearances, there's nothing untoward happening here. But if I assist a teenager in changing her clothes, the woman at the register won't let that slide. The cops would arrive faster than I could say human trafficking.

I wait in the hallway just outside the women's restroom for a while. Soon, the aroma drifting from the adjacent McDonald's calls to me. My stomach growls loudly, so I decide to step into the restaurant. She can find me after changing. And if she doesn't? Well, I've already done more for this stranger than many would.

I still don't know her food preferences. Guessing, I order fries and a cheeseburger for her, and a Big Mac for myself. With the food in hand, I settle at a table within view of the hallway linking McDonald's to the convenience store. As I eat, I intermittently glance up to check for her. Fifteen minutes pass, and I begin to doubt she'll join me.

A shiver runs down my spine.

She can't leave. She must come back.

The thought jolts me, nearly causing me to drop my burger. Wasn't I just thinking how nice it would be not to worry about her? The dread gripping my chest feels alien.

Then, abruptly, the girl appears and takes the seat across from me. The dread evaporates instantly.

The new clothes don't fit well. The gray sweatpants are rolled up around her ankles, the black university T-shirt hangs loosely from her shoulders, and the green hoodie is wadded into a ball that she holds tightly to her stomach. I don't see what she has done with her old clothes; perhaps they're rolled into a ball inside the hoodie.

I slide the tray toward her.

"I got you a burger and fries. Wasn't sure about your drink, so I left it empty," I explain.

She takes the paper cup and inspects it curiously. I point to the fountain drinks by the trash cans. As she gets up, she hands me a balled-up bundle of clothes. The girl peers inside the empty cup, then at me, and points to the fountain drinks. I nod. Either I'm getting used to her offbeat method of communicating, or she's adapting to mine.

Glancing at her as she walks away from the table, I quickly unwrap the clothes. Her uniform is neatly folded inside the hoodie, confirming my suspicion about the missing crest. If it's a school uniform, there's no clue as to which school she attends.

Her shoes squeak on the floor, and I hastily bundle up her clothes again. She returns with her drink and sits down. I casually place her clothes on the chair beside me and resume finishing my fries.

She watches me eat. I'm not usually self-conscious, but having someone silently observe as I shovel food into my mouth is unnerving. I forget my discomfort when she starts unwrapping her cheeseburger. I wonder if she'll actually eat this time.

She does. She eats the burger and fries, alternating between bites of one and handfuls of the other. I can't help but smile.

Grabbing a napkin from the tray, I pull a pen from my jacket pocket. The moment the pen clicks, her hazel eyes flick up to meet mine. Brown merging into green with a hint of orange—a detail I hadn't noticed before.

"You know how to write?" I lay the napkin flat and scribble in the corner to start the ink flowing. "I can believe you're mute, but these days, almost everyone can write, even if it's not perfect."

I place the pen on the table and slide it toward her. "Tell me something about yourself. Your name, where you're from, where you're headed. Anything. Or if you prefer, draw me a picture."

She picks up the pen and studies it closely, a habit I've noticed she has with most things. Like me, she scribbles in a corner of the napkin, pulling it closer and using her arm to hold it down, hiding her writing from my view.

My meal is finished; I had a head start while she was in the restroom. I sip my Coke while I wait. The pen scratches against the cheap napkin, and she glances at me occasionally before returning to her task. I raise an eyebrow. Is she writing an essay?

She continues for another few minutes, then places the pen down and lifts her arm, revealing the napkin. I squint at it. She hasn't written anything—it's a drawing. Well, I did suggest that as an option. For a moment, I can't make out what it is. Only when I rotate the napkin do I realize I was looking at it upside down.

It's a bird, crudely drawn but recognizable. Wings spread wide, a long beak with a slight hook at the end. My left hand unconsciously goes to my right wrist, rubbing the skin there.

"What does this mean?" I ask.

She doesn't respond, focusing on her fries and the straw in her cup. I sigh and put the pen away. So much for a breakthrough in communication.

Once we finish eating, we leave through the McDonald's side. She walks close beside me, carrying her extra clothes bundled up. The temperature has warmed since morning; I'd guess it's in the mid-sixties, warm enough for me to toss my jacket into the back of the truck.

A family is seated at one of the outdoor tables. One of the adults appears to be a woman about my age, accompanied by an older woman—I assume the mother and grandmother of the three kids with them. The two older boys, around seven or eight years old, are play-fighting with action figures more than eating. In a stroller sits a toddler, a girl with a small pink bow in her hair, munching from a green plastic container filled with dry Cheerios, which she scoops into her mouth by the handful. Just as many Cheerios end up on the ground as in her mouth.

A fleeting smile crosses my face before faltering. The girl beside me also notices the family at the table. I pause, realizing she's lagging behind and staring at the toddler with a quizzical tilt of her head. When the baby notices the girl, she returns the same curious gaze. In that moment, they seem so alike that I almost chuckle. The girl squats down and picks up one of the dropped Cheerios from the sidewalk. For a moment, I wonder if she's going to eat it herself, but then she holds it out to the toddler.

My heart skips a beat. I lurch forward to intervene just as the toddler starts to cry, catching the mother's attention as well.

"Excuse me!" She lunges for the girl and smacks the Cheerio out of her hand. "What do you think you're doing?"

I rush over and grasp the girl's arm, pulling her to her feet. "I'm sorry!" I apologize with a smile. "She's harmless, my niece." Lowering my voice, I add, "She's a little slow, though."

The mother hovers protectively over her child, her anger now tinged with embarrassment. She takes in the girl's loose clothing, the greasy sheen of her hair, and the blank look in her eyes. Slowly, her initial protectiveness fades, replaced by shame at having publicly scolded a disabled girl. Honestly, I would react the same way if I thought my child were in danger.

"Okay," the mother says, pulling the stroller closer. The toddler continues to cry. "Just don't hand things to babies off the ground. Understand?"

I tighten my grip on the girl's arm. "Yes, she understands," I assure the woman. "Again, I'm sorry about that."

I guide the girl away. She looks back at the family until they're out of sight. When we reach my parked truck, I take her by the shoulders and turn her to face me. There's no emotion on her face—no confusion, fear, anger, or embarrassment. Nothing. I should tell her off her, explain why she shouldn't approach other people's children without permission.

Instead, I ask, "You're not actually slow, are you?"

It's hard to tell. If she is, I should definitely take her to the police before accusations of kidnapping arise—or worse. Scratch that. I should take her to the police *regardless* of her mental capabilities. The thought of it, though, fills me with anxiety, every muscle tensing.

Her response to this question is the same as to every other. She takes her bundle of clothes to the passenger door and waits for me to unlock it.

"Seriously, kiddo. If you understand what I'm saying, you have to help me out."

I give her a stern look. She remains silent.

* * *

When my foot starts to cramp, I pull into a rest stop. "I need a break from driving," I tell the girl. "If you need to pee or stretch your legs, now's the time."

She follows me out of the truck and into the building, almost heading into the men's restroom with me.

"Whoa, no." I stop just outside the door and turn her towards the women's restroom. "I'm already taking a risk by not handing you over to the authorities. I won't make things worse. Go in there."

Clutching her oversized shirt, the girl suddenly seems much younger than fifteen. It's like I'm her dad, leaving her in a strange place, and she's unsure whether to cry or cling to my leg. It's surprisingly human for someone who has been emotionless until now. I place a hand on her shoulder. She twists the fabric of her shirt and looks up at me through dark lashes.

"Hey. We'll meet back here, okay? If I finish first, I'll wait for you. I won't leave you alone. Sound good?"

She nods once, the fourth time she's directly responded. We part ways. I head into the men's room, use one of the cleaner urinals, and try two sinks before finding one with soap. White suds pool as I rub my hands together. The scent of public restroom soap lingers.

My thumb skates over the inside of my right wrist as I rinse. Finally, I face the mirror. Yikes, I look rough. What was scruff along my jaw is now a full beard. Just call me Lumberjack Wolf. My hair is dark with grease from three

19

days without a shower. It might be oilier than the girl's. Bags hang under my exhausted gray eyes. I could really use a full night's sleep.

What about sleeping arrangements with Little Miss? The cheapest option is one room with two beds. I can't afford two rooms after buying overpriced clothes. The other option is a rest stop and sleeping in the truck, but that's uncomfortable. Whatever tonight's decision, I don't foresee the girl complaining.

I hang my shirt on a stall door and grab more soap to wash my upper body. Soapy fingers scrub my scalp and underarms, followed by a quick rinse and a pat dry with paper towels. My shirt feels nasty now that I'm partially clean.

Exiting the restroom, my right calf twinges, urging me not to rush back to the road. Two cars have joined mine in the parking lot. A family of six bursts in, four kids running. A boy and girl mimic race car noises, while harried parents handle a baby carrier and a diaper bag.

The women's door creaks open. It's not the girl, but two college-aged women, their heads bent together as they whisper. They seem bothered. Baby Carrier Mother passes them for the restroom with her infant. One of the young women pulls her aside.

"Don't use this one," she says. "We were just in there with a really weird girl. Bad vibes."

The mother seems startled by the strangers' advice. Her eyes dart between them, the restroom, and her baby. "Oh, um, thanks, but I need the changing station."

"We thought you should know," the second woman says. With a tight smile, the mom slips past them. The restroom door shuts, and the baby begins to wail.

A minute or so later, the door swings open again. For a moment, the baby's cries grow louder. Then the girl scoots through the narrow opening, letting the door swing shut in her wake.

She didn't clean up like I did. What was she doing there? She has to be as ripe as me, although I can't smell any body odor on her.

"Come on." I nod at the glass doors. "Let's walk."

3

Four and Twenty Blackbirds

I've tried to forget you, really, I have. Every time I think I've succeeded, something happens that reminds me of you. Mostly, it's the crows. I can't seem to escape them. One or two don't bother me, but when they gather together—that's what I can't stand.

Whose idea was it to call a group of crows a murder? Could they have chosen a more sinister word for a bird that already has a historically unsavory reputation? Their shiny black feathers move in a sea of squabbling birds, like a cluster of bees crawling all over each other. That's how I see those feathers—they come together to create a shiny, black, cawing hive.

Then suddenly they all take to the air, like an airborne disease. My skin crawls just thinking about it. Crows never used to bother me, not until the night of October 15. I have you to thank for that irrational fear. My therapist refuses to call it irrational, but I can read between the lines. What he doesn't understand is that I'm not afraid of crows. I'm disgusted by them. I itch to bash in their skulls. That's not fear. Here's what I'm afraid of: despite my revulsion, I'm afraid the crows will disappear and that I'll forget.

I don't hate you. I don't want you to think that. The problem is my feelings are contradictory—disgust and nostalgia, drawn and repulsed. I want to forget, yet I'm afraid. I wish I'd never met you, and yet I pray that you're dead. I wish you would come back.

I want to blame you for everything that's happened since you vanished, but it's *not entirely your fault. Don't get me wrong, a lot of it is definitely your fault. Just not all of it. This turbulence inside of me was brewing long before we met. You were just the one who unleashed it.*

* * *

The scenery surrounding the rest stop is breathtaking. Many trees are painted in fall colors, their leaves dropping to blanket the grass. Clouds have rolled in, obscuring the sun and casting everything in a dull light. Even the air is enticing, sweet with the slow decay of leaves.

Our feet crunch softly on the ground. With the sun gone, the temperature feels nippier than it did at lunch. Before our little excursion, we make a trip to the truck so the girl can throw on her green hoodie. She walks beside me, hands tucked inside the pouch.

A caw overhead has me tipping my chin up. A smattering of crows creates black dots against the slab of gray sky. They circle the area, probably hoping to find food left behind by humans.

"All right, missy," I say, trying to sound authoritative but feeling more like that bachelor uncle who can't discipline a child. Kids have a talent for sniffing out adults who lack the authority they should wield with age. "We need to find a way to communicate. Because this," I wave my hand between us, "ain't workin' for me."

The girl looks up, her gaze not on me but on the crows swooping through the air. Suddenly, a huge smile spreads across her face. It's so disarming that my stride falters. She keeps walking, putting a little spring in her step, and throws her arms out wide, twirling in circles. Her dyed black hair flies around her head like a dark halo. She resembles some kind of autumn spirit, embodying the overcast sky, the grass and trees, and the crows all at once.

She spins and spins. Her black hair gradually turns golden brown, her baggy clothes transform into a wavy dress, her pale skin darkens to a sun-kissed hue, and freckles bloom across her cheeks. My mouth goes dry. The way she appears now, this isn't the girl I've known, yet I recognize her. I'll always recognize her. I can't see her eyes from here, but I know they're sky blue. She collapses in the grass, causing my heart to stutter. My legs move instinctively before I realize what I'm doing.

She lies on her back, cushioned by red, orange, and yellow leaves. Directly in front of her, I see that it's the girl again. Dyed black hair, pale complexion, hazel eyes. She wears the clothes from the convenience store. Only then does my heart slow to a regular resting rhythm.

"You okay?"

I sound like I just sprinted fifty yards rather than crossing the seven feet between us. She doesn't answer, though she still bears the hint of that brilliant smile. The longer she gazes up at the cloudy sky, the more lost she begins to look. I watch the joy fade until her familiar blank expression is fully restored.

"You're not hurt, are you?"

I'm just talking to myself at this point. Sinking into a crouch, I drop down to my knees. The soft earth cushions my weight. My knees creak and pop in protest, reminding me that my body is almost forty, no matter how young my spirit feels. Moving slowly so I don't startle her, I extend a hand and touch her ankle. Gently squeezing and prodding, I conclude that nothing feels broken. If she is hurt, a twisted ankle is most likely. She seems fine, though. Physically, anyway.

I relieve my knees of pressure by shifting into a seated position on the ground with my legs crossed. Resting my arms on my thighs, I pluck a blade of grass carefully so that it doesn't snap. When it pops free, I turn it over to see the white end of it.

"What happened in the restroom?" I ask quietly.

She won't tell me, but her reaction might give something away. This is the second time a baby has cried near her. I can't say definitively that she caused of the most recent infant's distress, but I also can't ignore the coincidence that she was in close proximity both times. Then there were those two women who warned the mother not to enter the restroom.

"You're not a normal kid, are you?"

Normal kids have names. Normal kids don't emerge from the darkness and climb into a stranger's truck without a word of explanation.

I watch her pull deeper and deeper inside herself. There is no more happiness in observing the crows. A heavy sigh leaves me feeling deflated. Not for the first time, I wonder what the hell I'm doing. This annual road trip hasn't deviated in the past seven years. I've never ditched Carson and skipped town. I've never seen a hitchhiker on this stretch of highway. Any other time I saw a kid or teenager that looked lost, I would have called the cops. Once upon a time, the police and I didn't get along—in fact, that's still true most of the time—but missing children isn't an issue that I'm willing to compromise with my personal prejudices. In this one instance, the boys in blue and I are on the same side.

At least, we should be on the same side. Why haven't I called the police?

A sensation ghosts over the sensitive skin on the underside of my wrist. Jerking away, I see the girl's arm resting next to her head. She drops her hand to the grass, sluggishly curling her fingers as if she is still stroking my wrist. Grunting, I struggle to my feet. I'm not twenty-something anymore, and today I feel it. I offer the girl a hand.

"Come on, missy. If I don't move around, I'm gonna fall asleep, and we've still got a ways to go."

She accepts my hand and allows me to pull her off the ground. The girl is light as a feather.

I try to hide my surprise when she continues holding my hand after she has her feet firmly under her. She lets me lead us around the quaint park, swinging our linked hands back and forth. I can't take my eyes off her. It's not like earlier when I was entranced by the smile lighting her features. This time, I'm not bowled over. There is a quiet sense of security that fills me when her fingers squeeze mine.

I don't notice that she has taken the lead until we somehow end up back in the parking lot. I blink, and there's my truck. A handful of crows have settled on and around it. They all take flight as we draw nearer. Caws punctuate the air, and two inky black feathers float downward. The other two cars are gone now, leaving us alone at the rest stop.

Alone.

The sensation of ice water trickling down my spine sends goosebumps across my skin. It's time to hit the road again.

* * *

We stop again to buy coffee and snacks. I'm not sure if it's because I'm a little hungry, if snacking is just something to keep me awake, or if I'm seeking the reassurance I felt when I saw the girl eating a burger. She finishes another bottle of apple juice and decides she likes trail mix. Seeing her lick salt off her fingers calms me.

Flipping through radio stations, I come across one playing "Sweet Home Alabama." When it gets to the chorus, I crank up the volume. With a smile, I sing along loudly and tap the steering wheel. From the corner of my eye, I notice the girl. Her trail mix is gone, and she sits quietly with her hands folded in her lap.

"Okay, missy." I raise my voice above the music. "I know I've got a few years on you, but last I checked, everybody knows this song."

No response whatsoever. She doesn't look at me. Her attention is focused out the window, looking skyward. I didn't really expect her to sing along, but it was worth a shot. When the song ends, I turn the volume down. Without a familiar song to occupy my thoughts, they drift to my mute passenger.

I can't keep calling her "the girl" in my head. It feels weird. I faced a similar dilemma in one of my previous jobs. I didn't learn the name of the guy in the cubicle next to mine in the first two weeks, even though we talked almost every day. Then two years went by—well past the point when it was socially acceptable to not know his name. I got away with not calling him anything at all when we chatted in the break room, but I still had to call him something in my own thoughts. I think I landed on the name Harry Potter Glasses since the guy wore round corrective lenses.

I can't call her by some distinguishing feature. She doesn't really have any, except for her silence. Calling her "kiddo" is too generic. Any kid could be kiddo. But "missy" can be an actual name. My mom used to call my sister "missy" when she was little. Somewhere along the line, I picked up the habit. Of course, if I'm turning into one of my parents, it has to be my mom.

I glance at the girl again. She could be a Missy, I decide. She could be anyone. She has one of those faces that seem to fit any name: Sarah, Madison,

Heather, Lizzie, Danny, Max, John, or Bobby. But whatever name I choose, I have to be consistent. I thought of Missy first, so Missy it is.

Who is Missy? She might be a student from a private school where uniforms are mandatory, or she might just like the schoolgirl aesthetic. She could be a runaway hitchhiking her way to a new life, maybe escaping an abusive home. What other reasons does a teenage girl have to wander a highway in the middle of the night? Perhaps "wandering" is the key word—she might have a mental disability and wandered away from her caretaker. Surely, someone has noticed her absence by now.

I don't know what to make of all this. I don't know what I'm going to do after October 15. Missy isn't a puppy that I can adopt on a whim. She isn't a stray dog that I can hand over to just anyone, either. No matter who I turn her over to, there will be questions. How did I meet this girl? Why didn't I report her sooner?

What do I say to that when the truth sounds so unbelievable?

I catch a glimpse of myself in the rearview mirror. I look like I'm about to start a brawl. My brow is puckered, drawing angry lines across my forehead. My eyes are flinty, ready to let sparks fly if anyone breathes on me. I don't just look angry, I look scary.

I make a conscious effort to soften the planes of my face. There's no sense in making Missy afraid of me. Not that she's noticed the tension in the truck. Her temple is pressed to the window, her eyes still pointed at the sky.

The road stretches ahead of us. I turn off cruise control as we approach the township of Wilson. With such a small population, it's not even a blip on the map. Here, we switch from Highway 65 to Highway 250. Instead of continuing northwest, we turn completely west and then shoot straight north. Gradually, I decelerate from seventy-five miles per hour to thirty as we reach the town limits. There isn't much to see in Wilson. It's just the elbow where two highways meet and nothing else. The only thing it offers is fuel at a decent price.

The gas station is old enough that I have to go inside to pay. I look over my shoulder to check on Missy one last time before leaving her in the parking lot. She's climbed into the bed of the truck and has her head tipped back.

Satisfied, I enter the convenience store.

An air of familiarity wraps me in a warm embrace as I step inside. I've been passing through Wilson and stopping at this gas station for years. Though I only see the employees for a few minutes once a year, I've started recognizing faces. They don't wear name tags, and I've never introduced myself. They haven't asked for my name, yet I sense a certain acceptance. Like a foreign entity grafted onto a host, I feel that I won't be rejected as long as I don't come on too strong.

The wallpaper reminds me of a kitchen in a country cottage. Next to the shelf of cigarettes hangs a framed painting of a wheat field, the stalks bending in the wind. Soft folk music puts the final touch on the place. It's the coziest gas station I've ever visited.

A young woman is posted at the register. I recognize her. Years ago, she was a teenager stocking the shelves and taking out the garbage. Age has made her face thinner, and there are a few fine lines around her eyes and mouth. When she parts her lips, I see the first signs of nicotine stains on her teeth. She's rail thin; her fingers and arms resemble toothpicks when she takes my card. In my memory, she is Missy's age, with baby fat rounding the edges of her frame. Her silhouette is much sharper now. Even her hair seems thinner. Fragile. The urge to ask if she's hungry is surprisingly strong. Great, I *am* turning into my mother.

Waiting for the ancient computer to finish the transaction, she turns her gaze to the window. A massive scar on the side of her neck and the underside of her jaw leaps out at me. The scar tissue is shiny shades of pink and silver, disappearing under the collar of her shirt. The damaged, puckered skin is clearly a burn scar. My Uncle Jeb had the same marks on his arm after he was injured in a kitchen accident at the restaurant where he used to work. The woman's scar doesn't look recent, but it's new to me.

I swallow and avert my eyes.

"You've got company this year." She smiles, turning away from the window as the computer wheezes a sigh. All I see is the scar. The machine spits out my receipt, and she tears it off. "Is that the same girl?"

I snatch the receipt and my card, mutter, "Thanks," and then bolt out the door.

The landscape is veiled in grayish-blue tones, and the scent of rain hangs in the air. The township of Wilson is settled on a flat expanse of land encircled by forest on all sides. Looking over the grassy plain, I see a hazy curtain falling from the sky in the distance. We're going to be driving directly into that wall of rain.

Tucking my wallet into my jacket pocket, I make my way back to the truck. Missy is seated in the bed, though she isn't watching the sky any longer. The truck is surrounded by crows. Her head and arms are draped over the side as she studies the birds. The crows caw indignantly at my approach, scattering and taking flight. Missy stands and jumps to the pavement.

"Need the restroom?" I ask gruffly.

Her answer is to climb into the passenger seat. I follow suit, slamming the door behind me and sending more crows flying.

Wilson has one main thoroughfare. It takes forty-five seconds to drive down it, unless the light catches me at the one and only intersection. Then it takes roughly a minute and a half.

The light turns red, and I slow to a stop.In that minute and a half, I see more crows than I can count. They're perched on streetlights, sidewalks, roofs, and dumpsters. At the intersection, I have a perfect view of a tall oak tree swamped in a mass of black feathers. A cacophony of high-pitched, aggravated shrieks comes from the oak. As the light changes to green, I realize that the horrendous sound is coming from a group of squirrels. The squirrels in the oak scream at the invading birds.

* * *

The rain hits us with a vengeance. Several miles from Wilson, we drive into the wall I spotted earlier. It's not just water; hail clinks on the roof and windshield. I can barely see five feet in front of me, so I pull onto a narrow side road and park under the branches of an evergreen tree.

Missy has her feet up on the seat, her knees hugged tightly to her chest. I could turn on the radio, but who knows if any station will come in clearly.

Plus, the rain and hail are so loud that they'd probably drown out anything that does come in. I feel like I should do something to distract her. The way she curls into herself, she looks afraid the roof will cave in. I've never been faced with comforting a teenager in the middle of a storm, but I do have experience comforting a child. Is it so different? I hum for a second, partially to find the right note but also to get her attention.

Then I begin singing the lyrics to "Down by the Bay." I watch the rain strike the windshield while I sing, pretending not to pay any attention to Missy. I surprise myself by how many lines of the old song I remember. I haven't thought about it in years. There was a time when I memorized every verse just to annoy my sister. I have no idea if the song is helping Missy at all or if I'm just confusing her. Regardless, I think it's helping *me*. The dark cloud that has been dogging me for days feels lighter.

Four verses in, I run out of steam. There's more to the song, but the words are fuzzy in my mind. I chance a look at Missy. She's sitting on her folded knees, staring at me blankly. At least she isn't curled into a ball anymore. I unbuckle so I can turn sideways.

"We're gonna play a game. And don't worry, it doesn't require talking." I hold my hands in front of me, palms up. Missy doesn't move. "Come on." I curl my fingers, indicating she should give her hands to me. "I'm gonna look like a twelve-year-old girl for even knowing what this is, so feel free to make fun of me."

A tiny frown creates one shallow crease between her eyes as she hesitantly extends her hands. I take them, mirroring my position so we can clap them together. Up, down, up, down. She quickly gets into the simple rhythm. I feel silly reciting the "Obo Shin Otten Totten" chant. In my defense, it's one of those rhymes that got stuck in my head for the next thirty years after I first heard it.

By chance, my hands are on the bottom when the count reaches ten. I yank them out of the way on her downward stroke. Her palms land on the cup holders between us. Confusion furrows her brow, and her bottom lip juts out.

"That's the game, kiddo," I chuckle. "If you're on the bottom when we get to ten, you try to avoid being hit by the other person. You win if they miss. Vice versa if you're the one on top."

Her confusion morphs into concentration. She's fast, I discover. Once she knows the objective, I can't catch her. More often than not, the game ends with the sting of her fingers slapping my palms at lightning speed or with me batting at nothing but air. I only win that first round.

I call off the game when my skin looks red and burned. She looks at me expectantly, probably wondering, *What's the bizarre man going to do next?*

Truth is, I'm out of games. But the "Obo Shin Otten Totten" ditty has me thinking of other old songs that are tucked away in the dusty recesses of my memory.

"Sing a song of sixpence," I sing, tapping the rhythm on the steering wheel as I continue with the song about a pocket full of rye. "Four and twenty blackbirds baked in a pie."

The look in Missy's eyes is unfathomable.

"You know this one? I'd be shocked if you did. The only reason I know it is because of my dad. He used to have these old folk songs rattling around in his head. He'd go through his day whistling and singing. At his retirement party, his coworkers said they'd miss that the most. Said the worksite was gonna be too quiet with him gone."

I resume singing. It's been so long since I heard this song, but the lyrics are still there. Despite the fact that I'm the one singing it, the second to last verse surprises me.

"The maid was in the garden," the verse starts. When I get to the part about a blackbird flying down to the maid and pecking off her nose, I almost choke on my own tongue. "Well, that's dark," I mutter. "This might be the first time I've really paid attention to the lyrics."

Singing a jaunty tune about a maid losing her nose to a blackbird is definitely not the way to go about comforting a young girl.

Lightning flashes, zipping between dark clouds. Distant thunder rumbles as I switch songs.

I start to sing "You Are My Sunshine." The song seems appropriate for the weather. While the chorus sounds cheerful, the verses are about pining for a loved one, begging them to return. My mom used to sing it to me and my sister, though I never understood why. Was she thinking about the day her children would leave her?

An ache pulses in my chest, and my voice gets sucked into the vacuum of a black void. The song peters out pitifully when I can't force any wind past my vocal cords. We sit in silence until the hail lets up. By then, I've managed to swallow the knot in my throat. Putting the truck in drive, I pull onto the main road.

"See, sweetheart? That wasn't so bad."

She doesn't look scared now. I don't believe she has been since we started playing that game. Still, there's something about this moment that feels delicate, something that either one of us could shatter. In this instance, I take a page out of Missy's book and drive on in silence.

4

A Candle to Light You to Bed

Nights are the worst. I can't pinpoint the first night I slept alone—it seemed to happen gradually—but I remember how those lonely nights felt. Especially when I was not only alone in bed, but also alone in the house. Nowadays, being alone feels natural, though no more enjoyable than when I first became single. The pain is just less acute now.

But when I think about you, that pain feels fresh again. I don't miss you at night, not even a little. During the day, nostalgia creeps in, but as soon as the sun sets, I remember why I sometimes wish you weren't around.

There's something about you that most people saw except me. Looking back, it seems like ninety percent of the people who met you were instinctively put off. How did you deceive me? Or perhaps you sensed that I was blind to what everyone else saw? Hindsight is twenty-twenty. Too bad I was blind in the moment.

Now, when I sit in the dark and think of you, a creeping unease takes over. It's not you personally that gives me the willies; I spent many nights in your presence without discomfort. It's the idea of you that haunts me—the version of you I glimpsed at the end. In the week we spent together, I thought I understood you. But in our final moments, you revealed someone else. A stranger behind the familiar mask.

That's what shakes me—the realization that I never truly knew you. It's like missing a step in the dark—a fleeting but terrifying moment of imbalance. That's how I felt when I finally saw what lay behind your blank expression.

Now I'm left with two versions of you: one real, one a reflection, and I can't tell

32

them apart.

These nights, alone at home, I feel shaken. My heart races, and breathing becomes difficult. I wonder which version of you was real.

Now, in the darkness, I wonder if I'm truly alone.

***

A light sprinkling of rain falls from the dark storm clouds as we stop at a motel for the night. The clock on the dashboard reads 7:30 p.m., though the sky looks like it's somewhere around midnight. I tell Missy to wait in the truck while I go into the office.

The motel is right off the highway. There are just enough lights in the area to illuminate the vacancy sign, but beyond that is thick darkness. Our room faces the green sign pointing toward Highway 250. The magic I felt watching Missy run after the crows at the rest stop feels like it happened days ago. The dull fall colors have been overlaid with black ink.

The key card for the room jabs my thigh from its place in the pocket of my jeans. I grab my gym bag of clothes from the backseat. I mean to grab Missy's clothes too—who knows, she might want them with her. But her old clothes aren't in the backseat when I poke my head in there. I shrug, figuring she must have snagged them when I wasn't looking.

She isn't holding her clothes when I meet her at the door. If they're not in the truck and she doesn't have them, then I have no clue where they went. Right now, it's a mystery that I can't be bothered to solve. Short of nuclear war, nothing is going to keep me from collapsing into bed.

Two queen-sized beds take up most of the space in our room. The colors and the pattern of the duvets are hideous. It's an assault of navy blue, dull green, purple, and brown that swirls together into one big mess. I'm tired, I've been cooped up in the truck for hours, and I've been eating junk food all day. The culmination of these things is a nauseating headache, and the duvets are not helping. Neither is the stale odor wafting up from the old carpet.

I throw my bag on the bed closest to the door. A TV and microwave sit on the dresser. My stomach growls, reminding me that we didn't stop for dinner. Skimming the pamphlet of takeout places in the area, I decide that pizza sounds good.

"You can have the shower first," I tell Missy. "I'm gonna order food."

I don't bother to ask what she wants. She isn't going to tell me, and so far, she's proven not to be a picky eater.

Missy disappears into the bathroom. The ceiling fan roars to life when she turns on the light. I call the number for the pizza place and order a large pepperoni pizza with onions and veggies, then rattle off the address for the motel. Transaction finished, I hang up and turn on the TV.

I can't imagine a place like this has cable. My chances of finding a program worth watching are slim, but I scroll through the TV guide anyway. There are plenty of infomercials and fishing programs. Fishing in real life barely holds my attention for more than fifteen minutes; I don't see how anyone can watch another person fish for a whole forty-five minutes. Eventually, I find a channel that is playing an old Hitchcock movie called *The Lady Vanishes*.

Missy exits the bathroom before the pizza arrives. Already exhausted, I know I'm not going to have the energy to shower later, and I really shouldn't put it off another day. Just because she doesn't say anything doesn't mean she can't smell me. Setting the remote on the nightstand between the two beds, I dig the cash out of my wallet and set it next to Missy.

"If the pizza gets here while I'm in the shower, use this to pay the guy." On a pad of paper, I write a note saying whatever change is left can be the delivery guy's tip. I rip the page off and set it on top of the money. "Give this to him too."

The ceiling fan in the bathroom drowns out the TV on the other side of the door. I start to undress, but something stops me. Once again, I think of when I was walking back to my truck on the side of the road, carrying a can of gas and a flashlight. One second, everything was normal, then the air changed and I knew something was different. It's a similar feeling now. Although, this feels more like something is out of alignment rather than a shift in the air.

The bathroom is small with all the standard motel amenities. A towel rack above the toilet, a narrow shower covered by a white curtain, and a dinky trash bin next to the door. Nothing is out of place. I peer into the trash bin and lift the toilet seat on a whim, but both are empty. Not knowing what else to do, I shove the nagging suspicion to the back of my mind and strip out of my dirty clothes. It's only when I pull the shower curtain aside that I realize what's bothering me.

The floor and the walls of the shower are dry. Come to think of it, I didn't hear water running or the toilet flush when Missy was in here—only the obnoxious ceiling fan. She didn't have a towel when she came out, and I don't see a used one in here. Was her hair even wet? If only I'd been paying more attention. If she didn't shower while she was in the bathroom, then what was she doing? My mind conjures an image of Missy just standing here, blank-faced, doing nothing for ten minutes. Goosebumps ripple across my body, though that might be due to the fact that I'm standing here naked instead of turning on the water and getting into the shower.

Anyway, it's not my business what she does or doesn't do in the bathroom. The relief of washing days' worth of sweat and dirt off my skin is indescribable. The only downside is Missy's presence in the other room. People are never more vulnerable than when they're naked or asleep. I don't consider myself shy or self-conscious, but for some reason, Missy's presence is palpable. It makes me want to pull the shower curtain securely around my body. I rush through washing my hair and running the bar of soap over my skin.

Putting on dry, clean clothes is almost as satisfying as that first moment I stepped under the hot spray. Once all my vulnerable bits and bobbles are covered, I'm able to fully relax. As soon as I open the bathroom door, I smell warm cheese, onions, and baked dough. Missy sits on the bed with the pizza box, her hands hovering over it, collecting the warmth radiating from the cardboard.

"Smells good out here." I rub the towel roughly over my hair before tossing it onto the counter by the sink. I point to the box. "You can eat if you're hungry. No need to wait for me." She lifts the lid, releasing a cloud of steam. The black-and-white movie shows a woman running up and down the corridors of the train, asking people if they've seen the old woman she was with. "Were you watching this?" I ask.

The smell of pizza calls to my empty stomach, so I pull a slice free of the pie. Missy follows suit.

"The only Hitchcock movie I've seen is *Psycho*," I continue. "I caught parts of the old *Alfred Hitchcock Hour* because my dad used to have it on DVD. Personally, though, I prefer *The Twilight Zone*."

She stares at me methodically chewing, pizza grease dripping down my fingers. We don't have napkins.

"Hang on a sec, kiddo."

I walk to the bathroom and return with a wad of toilet paper. After wiping the grease off my hand, I tear some off for Missy. I give up on speaking after that; I feel like I'm talking to myself. As my mom used to say, "Talking to yourself is the first sign of madness," despite her own habit of chatting to no one while vacuuming.

The movie isn't bad; it's not a horror movie like *Psycho* but a gaslighting mystery. Between us, we polish off the pizza before the movie ends. Another old, black-and-white movie starts after the credits roll for *The Lady Vanishes*. My head nods, eyelids droop, and I miss the title. Shaking awake, I grab the remote and set a ninety-minute timer.

"If you can't sleep with the light or noise," I tell Missy, pulling down the sheets, "feel free to turn off the TV before the timer ends."

I ensure the remote's within her reach. Missy is on top of the ugly duvet, watching me prepare for bed. Muttering an awkward goodnight, I pull the lamp cord, plunging the room into darkness pierced only by the pale TV light.

* * *

I have that nightmare again—the one where I'm in the passenger seat of my truck and suddenly realize I don't know who's driving. The fear paralyzes me. Even though I know I'm dreaming, it doesn't change anything. I've only had one other lucid dream, and in that one, I felt a sense of freedom. I wasn't bound by what was happening in the dream; I was free to wake up.

In this dream, however, there's no freedom. I remain frozen, terrified to see the face of the driver but powerless to prevent my head from slowly turning. Like the first dream, the only detail I can distinguish is the outline of a body, the rest obscured in shadow. It looks like the person is wearing a hood. The only light comes from the dashboard and a sliver of moon in the sky—barely enough to see the driver's feet working the pedals. We're driving without headlights too.

Movement catches my eye outside the window. Shadows are falling from the sky. No, not from the sky—from the trees. I squint, thinking all the leaves are falling at once. But they're not leaves either. Black feathers are falling from the branches.

I don't wake up with a gasp. I don't thrash around in the sheets. Coming to is gradual. The motel pillow pressed to my cheek smells like stale cigarettes and a strong floral odor meant to mask the former scent. The room is pitch black.

My chest feels tight, as if my shirt is strangling me. My heart races as if it's beating sixty miles an hour. It takes ten minutes or more before my brain convinces my body it's safe to move. More than anything, I want to turn on a light to banish the darkness. But I hesitate, not wanting to wake Missy. A few more minutes pass before I feel I can sit up without risking a heart attack.

It was just a dream, I tell myself. Just a dream.

I lower my legs over the edge of the bed. The rough carpet touches the soles of my feet, and the blankets slide off me as I stand. Tiptoeing past Missy's bed, I head to the bathroom to relieve myself. Since I don't want the noisy ceiling fan to turn on, I decide to only turn on the light by the sink. There's a quiet click, and then my face appears in the mirror.

Even freshly showered, I don't look great. I look haggard. Beaten down. Defeated. And I still need to shave.

I go to the bathroom quickly, in the dark, and then return to the sink to wash my hands. There's no hand towel by the sink, but then I remember that I tossed the towel I used for my shower somewhere on the floor. Just as I bend down to retrieve it, something in the mirror catches my eye.

The duvet on Missy's bed is tucked in around the pillows just like it was when we arrived. Undisturbed. More importantly, the bed is empty.

Quickly, I run to turn on the lamp. She isn't anywhere in the room. It's impossible for her to be under one of the beds since there is no space between the frames and the floor. I press my hands to the spot where she was sitting when I went to sleep. It's cold. There isn't even an indent where her body was, so she hasn't been in bed for quite some time.

Muttering under my breath, I throw on my jacket and pocket the room key. The temperature has dropped to the low forties during the night. If I wasn't awake before, I am now.

First, I get the flashlight out of my truck. Then I proceed to search the parking lot. I shine the light under every single vehicle. No sign of Missy. I do a lap around the building, shining the beam into shrubbery and the woods. Still no Missy.

Next, I barge into the office. The ring of the bell on the counter is shrill as I push the button over and over. I'm sweating and on the verge of a panic attack by the time someone on the graveyard shift answers my call.

"Can I help you, sir?" The man pulls his head back as if stifling a yawn.

"Have you seen a young girl, a teenager? She has dyed black hair and was wearing gray sweatpants and a dark green hoodie."

I hate this feeling—out of control, yanked around like a dog's chew toy. It's like everything is conspiring against me, forcing me to acknowledge that no one really knows what they're doing. Sometimes, there isn't someone who has the answer, and I'm left with no one to turn to. I hoped I would never feel this way ever again, and now this happens.

Have you seen a young girl, I hear my past self say, *eight years old? She has light brown hair, and she's wearing ... What was she wearing?*

The man's eyes move from my face to something behind me. "Is that her?"

Following the trajectory of his finger, I whirl around. A vending machine is situated by the front door. Missy is six inches away from the glass, looking at all the snacks. I must have walked right past her when I came storming in.

Seeing her alive and unharmed makes the room stop spinning. My stomach feels sour, and my head is light and dizzy. I march to the vending machine, grab her by the arm, and spin her to face me. She isn't alarmed, surprised, or outraged at being manhandled. Her facial muscles are slack.

"What were you thinking?!"

She wasn't thinking, I try to reason with myself. She's a teenager who made an impulsive decision to leave the room in the middle of the night. There's something welling up inside me, though, that's ready to boil over.

"You didn't even take the key with you! How were you going to get back into the room?"

Her teeth clack together as her head snaps forward. The sane part of me is having an out-of-body experience, watching myself shake Missy. The rational part of my brain screams, *Stop! Someone else is in the room!* I'm ashamed that the only reason I pry my hands from her arms is the knowledge that the man behind the front desk looks ready to tackle me in about five seconds. The panicked, angry ringing in my ears slowly fades.

Missy's eyes are wide, and her shoulders are hunched. She shrinks away from me as soon as I release her. The sick feeling in my gut resurfaces but for an entirely different reason.

I drop my head into my hands, pressing the heels of my palms into my eyes. "I'm sorry," I murmur. "I'm sorry, sweetheart. I woke up, and you were gone, and I didn't know if something had happened or…"

Or what? I thought I didn't care if she left. I thought I didn't want her to be my problem, but I'm starting to remember what it feels like to not be alone all the time. Do I really want Missy to leave now?

Small arms wind around my waist. Her cheekbone comes to rest against my ribs. Lowering my hands, I see spots at first, but when my vision clears, the crown of Missy's head is directly in my line of sight. Her ear is positioned over my heart.

"Everything all right?" The man behind the desk has relaxed his stance. I wonder what would have happened if Missy's display of affection hadn't put him at ease.

"Yeah," I say. "My niece just gave me a scare. Her mom would kill me if I let anything happen to her."

The guy nods. "I hear ya."

Missy pulls back and takes my hand, leading us out of the office. We're almost back to our room, so I dig in my jacket pocket for the key. "If you were hungry," I say to her, "you could have woken me."

She shrugs. It's barely a response, but it raises my spirits.

We enter the room, and I watch as she walks to her bed and lies on top of the duvet. Exhaustion hits me like a train. All I want to do is collapse on top of the covers like Missy. Instead, I ask her, "Are you hungry? I think I have some change in my wallet. I can go back to the vending machine."

Missy shakes her head.

Sluggishly, I get ready for bed again. I kick off my shoes, put the room key on the dresser, and toss my jacket over the chair. On goes the TV, and I set the timer once more. I'm so tired that I probably don't need anything to fall asleep to, but I fear that if the silence settles in, it might smother me.

Already half asleep, a thought pops into my head. Missy's bed was cold when I checked it. She couldn't have been standing in front of that vending machine for very long if the guy on the graveyard shift hadn't noticed her. Where else did she go? Something tells me I should stay awake and wait for her to fall asleep, except I can't keep my eyes open. When my eyelids fall shut, Missy is still staring at the ceiling.

* * *

I feel like an even bigger jerk the next morning. I can't believe I shook her. Yes, I was scared, but that's no excuse.

Missy is already awake by the time I get up. Just like last night, she lies flat on her back and stares at the ceiling. Once I'm on my feet, she trails after me while I get ready for the day. I dig inside my bag until my fingers close around plastic. "Here." I give her my spare toothbrush. "You can have it. Don't worry, it's new. I carry that with me when I travel, just in case."

It feels strange standing at the sink with someone by my side. We're elbow to elbow in front of the mirror, both brushing our teeth in small circles. I spit and rinse off the bristles.

"Sorry about last night," I finally manage to say. "I shouldn't have lost my temper."

Missy meets my gaze in the mirror. Then she bends over and copies my actions, spitting and rinsing.

"It's not going to happen again," I assure her. "Promise."

I can't tell if she's mad at me. The hug last night suggests that she isn't, but she might have just been scared and trying to calm me.

She watches me while I put our stuff together until the moment that I usher her outside. Mist hangs in the air, and my breath fogs. I leave her in the truck when I go to check out. Seeing the vending machine in the office reignites the guilt weighing heavily in my stomach. It's not the same guy at the desk this morning, but I still feel like he knows what went down last night.

Once everything is squared away, I set a brisk pace for the truck.

"You want breakfast, kiddo?" I shut the door and turn the key in the ignition. "Waffles, pancakes, bacon? Any of those sound good to you?"

I look at her earnestly, hoping she sees my sincere apology. Her expression is devoid of emotion, just like every other time I've interacted with Missy. However, this time feels different, like I've been digging a hole and just realized it's too deep to climb out of on my own.

I am in so much trouble.

"Well, it sounds good to me. Let's get some grub."

5

Silver Bells and Cockleshells

There are moments in any relationship that stand out, like how a parent fondly remembers their child's first word. The same child says many more words in later years—too many to count, and many that shouldn't have been said. But there's something special about that first word. The last words are significant as well, but ideally, parents don't live to hear their child's final words.

I think firsts and lasts are the most memorable moments. Any moments in between have to do something to stand out from the crowd.

You were good at standing out.

I haven't figured out why you didn't talk right away. I have theories, though. Some make a certain amount of sense, while others are off-the-wall batty. I'll start with the craziest one that not even I really believe.

You were an alien, new to Earth, and you didn't know any human languages, so you learned from listening to me talk. You soaked up words from the radio, from the TV, and from strangers. You hoodwinked me somehow, or my own emotional baggage blinded me to any signs that you weren't human. Other people saw it in you—the babies you made cry, the kids you frightened, the adults you flustered.

My second theory is that you had the ability to speak from the beginning but chose not to. You were just really good at playing the role of a helpless little girl, and you furthered that image by pretending to be mute.

Here's my third and final theory about the silence you perpetuated in the beginning.

People say a lot of words. It's impossible to remember them all, no matter how much we love or hate someone. I think there was something you wanted me to remember. Something that you said. You had to be sure I didn't forget it, so you couldn't say any words that didn't matter. I've got to hand it to you; it was a good strategy. I remember everything you told me. The problem is that I don't know what to do with that information. You could have been less cryptic.

My belief is that the mystery ultimately boils down to the first thing you said. First words are important.

I'm aware that I sound like a loony conspiracy theorist. I know what people say about me, and maybe they're right. But I just can't let this go.

* * *

We get breakfast at a Perkins. The two of us order waffles, bacon, and eggs. I don't know how she likes her eggs, so I get her the same as me.

Despite still feeling remorseful about shaking her and yelling at her, my frustration with her doubles back fast. If we can't find some way to communicate, I'm going to lose my mind. I always wondered how some parents could get so frustrated with their kids that they lost all reason and hit them. I don't smack kids for any reason, but I'm starting to understand a little more. Even though the guilt of last night is simmering, I also kind of want to shake Missy again until she makes some sort of human noise.

Maybe she really is afraid of me. Who wants to talk to a guy that frightens them? Nobody. Showing her some of my own vulnerabilities might help. It certainly can't make things worse.

I glance at my phone to check the time, only to see that it's powered off. Huh, I guess I did that after Sycamore. That explains why I haven't heard from Carson. Turning it on, I see five missed calls, all from him. I'll call Carson back in a little while. It's 8:40, so we'll get to Birchwood Lake today, probably by this afternoon.

"Snakes," I say. Missy stops chewing, swallows, and looks at me. "I'm afraid of snakes," I clarify. "Me and Indie, we're on the same page. Snakes are gross. I don't like the way they move."

I push the leftover syrup around my plate. Missy blinks, then takes her fork and copies what I'm doing. I have to bite my tongue to stop myself from fishing for information. I'm supposed to be showing her one of my vulnerabilities, not interrogating her. As always, she stays silent.

Our server returns and offers to refill my coffee cup. Missy stares at me, ignoring the server when he asks if she wants anything else. Interceding, I request another apple juice for her. He smiles and takes our empty plates when he leaves. Without syrup to fiddle with, I start ripping a paper napkin, tearing it into thin ribbons.

"You have a bird on your skin."

My fingers pause. There are a few other people in the Perkins, but none of them seem to be paying attention to us. I run the pad of my thumb over my wrist. It sounds like a girl talking, but the only person giving me her full attention is Missy.

"Well, I'll be damned." I cross my arms and lean forward. "She speaks."

Missy mimics me, folding her arms on top of the table. "I can talk."

Her voice isn't what I expected. I thought it would be higher, something younger and more naive. Instead, her soft voice isn't the least bit hoarse, despite her days of silence. She speaks in a lower register, making her seem older in an instant.

"Now that the cat's let go of your tongue, I don't suppose you're gonna tell me your name or where you're going."

Our server returns and sets another glass of apple juice in front of Missy. He refills my coffee with a friendly smile and asks if we need anything else. I say no more curtly than necessary; he might have just ruined my chance to discover who this girl is.

The server leaves, and I turn back to Missy. If she intended to answer my question before we were interrupted, she doesn't look like she will now. She sucks apple juice through the straw with enthusiasm. Well, so much for that.

I sip my coffee slowly, reluctant to leave the restaurant in a hurry. I get the feeling that as soon as we get back in the truck, her voice will disappear again. "It's an albatross," I say, hoping to keep her engaged by talking about my tattoo, the one thing that seems to interest her. "Do you know anything about albatrosses?"

She sits back in her chair, letting her hands fall in her lap.

"An albatross can fly ten thousand miles just to feed their young," I tell her. "And sailors used to see them as a sign of good fortune."

We stare at each other for a minute. I'm tempted to say more—ask her why she noticed my tattoo, if she likes birds. But something tells me to be patient. She's been mirroring my actions, so it might be a good idea to copy hers for once. So, I stare back at her just as intently and silently.

She has remarkably clear skin for a teenager on the run—no blemishes, moles, or freckles in sight. Her skin looks so smooth that I imagine it could shatter like porcelain. I clench my hands around my coffee cup. Heat radiates from it, soaking into my skin—skin that is not like porcelain. I am weathered, beaten leather to her glass.

"It's a paradox."

My head snaps up again, my attention zeroed in on her. "What's a paradox?"

She nods to my wrist. Letting go of my cup, I lay my hand on the table, palm up, so she has a better view of my tattoo. Missy tilts her head, studying the inked bird on my arm.

"An albatross," she says. "It's good luck, but it's also a burden and a curse." Her hazel eyes grow wide. "A paradox, and you put it on your skin."

One of my eyebrows arches. I have a vague recollection of reading "The Rime of the Ancient Mariner," which makes mention of the albatross being burdensome. I had to read it in college. Did that poem somehow become standard reading for the ninth grade? She regards my tattoo with single-minded concern, as if I've done something highly questionable and she is trying to understand why.

I pick up my coffee cup and motion to her juice. "You should finish that. We'll have to be outta here soon."

I gulp down a scalding mouthful of coffee, and Missy does the same with her juice.

***

She has yet to tell me when she needs the restroom, so, just to be safe, I pull into a gas station outside of Birchwood Lake.

"I'm gonna buy a pack of gum," I tell her. "While I do that, you should use the restroom."

I kind of feel like I'm babying her, but if she prefers otherwise, she should speak up more—now that I know she can speak. She doesn't give me any guff before wandering off in search of the restroom.

Though we're near Birchwood Lake, the secluded lake won't come into view until we're deeper into town. Birchwood Orchard offers a stunning overlook. Perched on a hill, the orchard, pumpkin patch, and cornfield provide a scenic backdrop. During the Fall Festival, visitors can relax with apple cider on the hill or head to the beach for live music.

For a day, time seems to stand still. The world beyond Birchwood Lake will disappear. Music plays endlessly; red leaves never fall; green grass remains ever vibrant. But once we leave town in the truck, reality resumes, and we'll die. After we die, the rest of the world will come back into focus. Time will start again, and everything will move forward. It's a day I eagerly anticipate each year, yet the thought of death fills me with dread.

I'm chewing a stick of spearmint gum when Missy rejoins me at the truck. I have no idea if she actually went to the restroom or simply stood around the corner doing nothing.

From that gas station, it takes us only twelve minutes to roll into the town of Birchwood Lake. It appears just as picturesque as ever, with its square storefronts reminiscent of bygone eras. The winding streets cut through wooded areas ablaze with maroon and gold hues. Tranquil neighborhoods exude serenity, their yards nestled snugly among the trees.

The motel I always stay at is close to the small library by the beach. There are two other cars in the parking lot. It's reassuring to see this place attracting other guests besides myself. I ask Missy to wait while I check in for a room. The young man at the reception desk, who checks me into Room 5, is unfamiliar. I noticed a few years ago that the residents of Birchwood Lake are beginning to change. It doesn't feel very long ago that I knew everyone in town. Now there are kids, teenagers, and young adults whom I've never seen before. While the town itself may remain unchanged, its inhabitants are evolving.

"This place is better than the other motel," I assure Missy as I unlock the door to Room 5. "And we're not far from the lake, so we can go wading in the water if you want. Although, the water is pretty cold this time of year."

Every room I've stayed in here has had a similar decor, reminiscent of a cozy log cabin with shades of dark wood and forest greens. I even find the tacky fish lamp on the nightstand charming. I drop my belongings on the bed nearest to the door. Missy stands quietly, taking in the room.

"I used to live here, you know." I mention. Missy turns to look at me. "In Birchwood Lake," I clarify, "not in this motel. I grew up here. My parents lived in the neighborhood west of this one, but they moved a few years ago. They offered to sell me the house, but..."

I realize too late that I've ventured into sensitive territory and should have stopped talking sooner. Fortunately, Missy doesn't press for details.

Clapping my hands together, I change the subject. "So, this is where my journey ends. Now would be a good time to tell me where you're going."

She sits on the other bed, examining the fish lamp curiously. The base of the lamp is shaped like a bass leaping out of the water. She pulls the cord, and yellow light pools on the nightstand.

"I'm with you," she says quietly.

Her verbal affirmation warms my heart. "Yeah, you are. But remember, this is where I stop. After October 15, I'm getting in my truck and heading home."

Missy pulls the cord again, switching off the lamp.

"I'm with you," she repeats more resolutely.

I sigh. "Fine. Only until October 15, though. After the Fall Festival, you'll have to tell me where you're goin' next, otherwise I'm taking you to the police."

She remains silent. Missy picks up the TV remote from beside the lamp and presses the power button. An ESPN commercial fills the room, and I begin unpacking but pause shortly after. A fleeting thought crosses my mind: she's doing exactly what I did. At the previous motel, one of the first things I did was turn on the television.

* * *

After lunch, I buy some crackers and take Missy down to the beach. This time of year, the lake is cold. My idea to go wading seems ridiculous once I dip my toe in the water lapping at the sand. I yelp and hop around, shaking my foot dry. I laugh it off as I jog back to where Missy sits in the sand.

"Forget it," I shiver. "Water's freezing."

I fall next to her on the soft ground. We're both barefoot, seated in the sand with the bottoms of our pants rolled up. The packet of crackers is between us. I tear the packaging open and grab a handful. Snapping one of them in half, I hurl the piece into the sand several feet away. In an instant, a group of seagulls descends, fighting for the snack. I throw the rest of the cracker into the squabble of birds.

With a smile, I extend the packet to Missy. "Wanna feed them? They're not scared of people. You can get them to come right up to you."

To prove my point, I break apart another cracker and sprinkle the pieces in the sand right in front of us. Five seagulls take notice and fly over without any hesitation. I could probably get them to take food from my hand, though that might incite a mob of birds to flock us. I keep the rest of the packet of crackers hidden behind me and discreetly offer it to Missy.

Her thin fingers gingerly pluck one cracker from the plastic. She does what I did, breaking the cracker into pieces and tossing them onto the sand in front of her. The nearest seagulls jump and stretch their wings. They eye the pieces of cracker with interest, but they don't move any closer. I frown and lean forward.

"That's odd. I've never seen a seagull turn down food, especially since they were all over the crackers I gave them." Testing a hunch, I throw another cracker onto the sand. The five birds close to us jump on it. Huh…

I give Missy another cracker. "Throw it."

She does. The seagulls look at it, then at Missy, and then peck at the ground where my cracker used to be. I raise an eyebrow.

"That's bizarre. Normally, they're not picky about who they take food from."

It's doubly strange given how friendly she is with crows. I remember how they flocked around my truck while she gazed down at them adoringly. While crows coexist well with humans, they tend to be wary of us. Seagulls, on the other hand, seem to have figured out that most people don't care enough to bother them. I imagine that if any bird were to approach Missy without fear, it would be a seagull. Even though they don't actively avoid her, they definitely don't want to approach.

She pulls her legs up, dragging her feet in the sand, and folds them under her. Only then do the birds hesitantly peck at the crackers she threw for them.

"What'd you do to scare the seagulls, Missy?" I nudge her playfully with my elbow.

I make sure to infuse some warmth into my smile in the hopes that she feels comfortable enough to talk to me again. My ex used to say that my smile is what reeled her in. And in a way, I am trying to reel in Missy.

"You're not afraid of snakes," she says. My smile drops.

"What?"

Missy looks up at me from beneath her dark lashes. "You're not afraid of snakes. No one is."

No one is afraid of snakes, huh? Try telling them that.

I snort. "Oh, yeah? How do you figure?"

Please, Little Miss, explain to me why my irrational fear doesn't exist.

Missy stares at the seagulls on the beach. "Everyone is afraid of the same thing, and it isn't snakes."

"What's everyone afraid of then?"

There is a long pause where I think she won't answer. Cries from the seagulls fill the air. A bunch of them take off, flapping to gain altitude, and then glide over the choppy waters of the lake. It's been so long since I sat on this beach. I can't remember the last time I did. For years, I sat here with warm bodies on either side of me. Then, for a while, I sat on the beach alone, lost. After a year or two of that, I stopped coming to the beach altogether.

"Everyone is afraid of being in the dark," she says, "and wondering if they're alone."

I come back to the present where Missy is sitting beside me. Her eyes are pointed straight ahead. A cool breeze whips her hair around her face, and limp, black tendrils caress her porcelain cheek.

"I know you're young and it doesn't seem like it," I say, "but most people eventually grow out of their fear of the dark."

Looking at her profile, I see one corner of her mouth pull up. It's barely a hint of a smile, but it sends a shiver coursing through my body in waves. This smile isn't the one I saw when she joyfully chased after the crows.

Without tearing her gaze away from the lake, she replies, "No, they don't."

We stay for a few more minutes even though I'm ready to go right after that conversation. However, I don't want her to think I'm upset with her, so I force myself to wait another five minutes before suggesting that it's time to leave.

My phone is in the truck where I left it. Missy is still in the grass, trying to rub the sand off her feet. I've been meaning to call Carson back ever since I turned my phone on again, but I keep forgetting. While I was on the beach, I see that I've missed two calls and a text message. None of them are from Carson. Exhaling through my nose, I select the number and press send. I only hear ringing for a second before the call is answered.

"Kevin?"

"Hey, sis."

Annika must have steam pouring from her ears if she's calling me. Disapproving and irate are the only moods she's ever in when she calls.

"Where the hell are you?! Carson's been blowing up my phone. He's worried sick because apparently, you've lost your damn mind!"

"I'm fine," I assure her. "I'm in Birchwood Lake, like I always am at the beginning of October."

"Well, Carson doesn't think you're fine. He says you made a scene when you showed up in Sycamore and then took off without a word."

"I didn't make a scene!"

What's he talking about? I think I kept my cool even when it was clear Carson thought I was so exhausted that I was hallucinating teenage hitchhikers. That was certainly no reason to throw me under the bus by calling my little sister.

"That's not the point, Kevin! He says he's been calling you nonstop for the last day and a half, and you haven't answered or called him back. And when I couldn't get in touch with you either, we were both ready to file a police report! What were we supposed to think? For all we knew, you were dead in a ditch somewhere."

Through the angry tirade, I hear Annika's voice crack on the word "dead." My indignation fades into sheepishness. I know she worries about me in her own way. Our mom worries too, and our dad would join the worriers' club if his mind wasn't stuck in the past. I hate that I make them feel like this. They don't need to worry about me, but I don't know how to express that to them. I don't know how to make them believe me.

"Obviously, I'm not dead," I say. "I'll call Carson and get him off your back."

"Kevin … there's one more thing."

That tone makes my heart skip a beat. It's a warning that bad news is coming. The last time I heard that tone was from a police officer. I think I took a swing at him, although I can't remember for sure. He didn't arrest me; he just left me to cry and destroy the house by kicking and punching holes in the walls. The last time I heard that tone from my sister, she was telling me that our parents were selling our childhood house and that our dad was moving into a nursing home.

"What?" I say past the knot in my throat.

"You weren't answering my calls or my texts." Annika already sounds defensive, and she hasn't even delivered the bad news yet. "I wasn't sure if something had happened to you."

"Annika, just tell me."

A beat of silence, and then, "I called Rebecca."

Without another word, I hang up on her. My fingers flex around my phone. I bite the inside of my cheek to keep from screaming and then throw my phone into the back of the truck.

She called Rebecca.

6

Lucy Locket Lost Her Pocket

To this day, I can't figure out what your game was. Were you selfish, only using me and others to get what you wanted? Or maybe there was a tiny shred of compassion in your heart. When I look back on your behavior, sometimes all I see is a remorseless, wild animal. But then I recall the way you stooped to pick up a fallen Cheerio to return it to a toddler with a bow in her hair. When I think of that, I don't believe you could have been entirely without empathy. Were people merely tools to you, or did you pity us? This is assuming you aren't human. If you are, then I'm even more confused. What happened to alienate you from the rest of us? Something must have happened to you. No teenager acts like you without dragging a whole collection of baggage behind them.

I'm glad I left you at the motel that night after Annika called. If I had been at the motel with you, I would have seen what you got up to. Not that I have proof you did anything wrong. You only left me with signs and suspicions. By the time the cops found that man's body—the man from the Blue Fox—and I put together the pieces of that night, it was two weeks later. By then, we were gone. I returned to my life, and you ... well, you just vanished.

* * *

I call Carson, assure him I'm fine, and then give him an earful for involving my sister. He doesn't sound remorseful until I mention she called Rebecca;

52

then he's at least somewhat apologetic. By the time I end the call, my blood pressure is dangerously high. Meanwhile, Missy has been sitting on her motel bed, watching me.

"Sorry," I say gruffly. "Family drama."

Running my hands over my face, I close my eyes and inhale the scent of the motel soap. If Annika decides I'm not okay, or if Rebecca feels obligated to intervene, the next four days won't be the relaxing getaway I've been hoping for. I trust Carson to back off now that he knows I've safely reached Birchwood Lake. My sister and ex-wife, however, are a different story.

Exhaling heavily, I drop my hands to my sides. Missy continues to watch me. I could really use a break from all this.

I retrieve my keys from my pocket and tell her I'll be back in a few minutes. Most kids would ask where I'm going or if they can come along, but Missy simply folds her hands in her lap. She doesn't acknowledge understanding, yet doesn't seem confused either. It's more than a little strange, especially now that I know she can speak without difficulty.

Exiting the motel room, I gently close the door. For a moment, I'm tempted to peek through the window to see if she's moved, but then a fear grips me: if I look, I might find her staring right back at me.

A shiver runs through me, which I blame on the crisp autumn chill. It's not even six yet, and the sun is already sinking below the trees. I get into the truck, crank up the heat, and pull out of the parking lot. There's only one pizza place in town. The food's decent, and it's not too expensive. I eat there every year, but tonight, pizza doesn't appeal to me. Still, I head there because I need to feed Missy.

As I drive across town, I ponder who Missy might be. Thoughts about her friends and family, and what they must be going through, flood my mind. I understand their feelings—the sense of helplessness, the guilt over not preventing her disappearance. They're scared and angry, grasping at any hope that she'll return. It's up to Missy. It's up to me.

If Missy were my daughter, I'd want whoever found her on the roadside to take her straight to the police. I'd dread hearing that tone of voice bringing bad news.

Then it hits me: Missy's parents might not think like me. Perhaps there's a reason she hid when I tried to hand her over to Carson. Maybe home isn't safe for her. Would involving the authorities send her back to a dangerous situation? I could unintentionally cause harm by alerting them to her whereabouts. The problem is, I don't have all the facts. A possible solution dawns on me: I'll try to convince her to call her parents. That way, I can observe their interaction and judge for myself if home is a safe place for her.

Taking one hand off the wheel, I massage my forehead. I don't know what to do. I know what I *should* do, but I don't know how to do it. I'm not sure why this is so hard. I didn't think twice the first time I considered taking her to the police. I actually attempted to do it, but ever since then, it's like I come up with new excuses not to. It's not typical of me to be paralyzed by indecision, especially when the answer seems so clear-cut.

The warm, garlicky scent of pizza seeps into the vehicle before I even get out of the truck. The place isn't particularly busy tonight. Through the windows, I see two teenagers and a larger group occupying four tables. The sign over the doorway says Alfred's Pizzeria. I remember coming here as a kid for family dinners, and then bringing dates here as a teen. Alfred's isn't very big. There are five tables, a counter by the windows, and a wall of arcade games. My mouth curls into an involuntary smile when I see the deer hunting game and pinball machine are still here.

I walk up to the register and wait for someone to take my order. At one time, I knew everyone working here and all the customers. Glancing at the occupied tables, I don't recognize anyone. The girl who comes to take my order has a brown ponytail pulled through the back of her green Alfred's cap. Her name tag says Liz. No last name, so I don't know if she has any family in town that I might remember.

Liz puts on a hospitable smile. "Hi! Welcome to Alfred's Pizzeria. What can I get you this evening?"

I don't know what kind of pizza Missy prefers. I know what kind I like, but I'm not planning to eat dinner with her. Part of me feels bad about that, but I remind myself I won't be very pleasant company tonight after that call from Annika. Really, I'm doing Missy a favor by giving her an evening to herself. She seemed okay with the pizza I ordered last time, so I choose an old favorite of mine: the pepperoni and veggie deep dish. I order it to go and lean against the faded wallpaper while I wait.

Above the noises from the kitchen and the various discussions at the tables, I hear faint riffs of blues music. This place really is a time capsule.

My phone buzzes in my pocket. Recent events have shown me that ignoring my phone is more trouble than answering it, so I fish for the device. It's a text from Rebecca: *"r u ok??"*

My throat constricts. Rebecca and I weren't on good or bad terms when we split. It wasn't that black and white. We just fell apart and then couldn't figure out how to make the pieces fit back together. Seeing and talking to each other these days is awkward.

I ponder what I want to say for a few seconds. Should I explain what's going on? I can't imagine she'll tell me to do anything I haven't already thought of, and I don't relish the idea of telling her why I can't do any of those things. I'm not even sure how to explain it to myself. Rebecca won't understand.

I tap the text field and a keyboard appears on the screen.

"i'm fine," I reply and hit send.

A moment later, my phone vibrates again.

"did u tak2 annika? seh soundd worryd"

I chuckle. At best, Rebecca's texts are recognizable as English. At worst, deciphering her texts is like translating a foreign language with zero grammatical rules to keep it consistent. I once timed myself; it took fifteen minutes to figure out the meaning behind an incomprehensible three-part message from her.

"Annika got ahold of me. everything's a-ok"

That seems to satisfy her, as my phone doesn't buzz a third time.

The pizza box is steaming when Liz sets it on the counter. I thank her, and she tells me to have a good night.

The steam rising off the cardboard box is tantalizing. My stomach growls all the way back to the motel. I'm tempted to stay in the room tonight and share this pizza with Missy, just to have a bite of deep-dish goodness. But then I recall my frustration with the one-sided conversations, the prickly sensation of being watched all the time. Tonight, I need to be around normal people—people who respond when I speak. I need small talk instead of cryptic lines followed by silence. Normality is what I crave right now, more than Alfred's pizza.

Entering the room, I notice the TV still on, but Missy is nowhere to be seen. I set the pizza box on her bed and peek around the corner. The bathroom door is shut, light seeping from underneath, and the fan hums steadily. I knock twice.

"Hey, kiddo? I got you pizza for dinner. I'm going out for a bit, but I'll leave you with a room key and my phone number. Okay?"

I don't wait for a response.

In the nightstand drawer, I find a pen and notepad. I jot down my number and leave it on top of the pizza box. Before leaving, I ensure the spare room key is on the dresser. Confident everything is in order, I call over my shoulder, "I'll be back later tonight!"

There's no response.

I close the door firmly behind me and return to the truck.

* * *

The Blue Fox Bar & Grill—no one really knows why it's called that—is on the outskirts of town. The parking lot smells heavily of smoke. Indoors, it's warm and loud, with a football game playing on the TV near the bar. The place is packed, so I grab the first empty table I see. A waitress brings me a beer while I wait for the burger I ordered.

And just like that, I'm alone again. Alone, but not being watched. It's not that I mind Missy watching me most of the time, but it starts to feel creepy after a while. It wouldn't be so bad if she talked more. As she's shown, though, I can't count on that. Tonight, I may not have any company, but it's nice to hear other people chatting.

"Can I sit here for a minute?"

I look up to see a girl standing by my table. She's dressed in a short, tight skirt and a top with a plunging neckline. Carefully crafted brunette curls frame her face, and she's wearing more makeup than anyone else here. Her nails are shiny and red. She looks young, like she can't be any older than seventeen.

"I'm meeting someone," she explains, "and I don't want to wait standing alone in a corner until he gets here. Shouldn't be more than five minutes."

I nod, and she flashes me a pretty smile. Chair legs scrape against the floor as she takes the seat opposite me.

"Hi," she says, offering her hand. "I'm Ginger."

Shaking her hand, I can't help but think of Missy. She and Ginger look almost the same age.

"I'm Wolf," I reply.

Ginger shifts, tilting her head down to look at me through mascaraed lashes.

"Wolf, huh? That's an interesting name."

"It's my last name."

She leans forward, pushing her arms together to emphasize her cleavage. "Can I tell you a secret, Wolf? Ginger isn't my real name."

I raise an eyebrow. "No kidding," I say dryly. "So, do you meet many guys in Birchwood Lake? Doesn't seem like a big enough town for ... whatever it is you do."

I almost slip and call her a prostitute, but I notice the dirty looks she's getting from other patrons and decide she might appreciate a bit of discretion. Not that she's being discreet herself. Behind all the eyeshadow, she seems like a teenager who may not grasp the future repercussions of her actions. If Ginger were in her twenties, I might not feel the same need to shield her from judgment. But I'm not sure she's even legal.

Ginger shrugs. "People in the country have needs too, and it's pretty easy to find guys online. Plus, the farther I have to drive, the more I can jack up the price."

She winks at me.

With a small smile, I shake my head. Having a teenage girl flirt with me is a heady mix of flattering and off-putting.

"Do you have any idea how old I am?"

"Age is just a number. It doesn't mean anything."

"I thought you were meeting somebody."

"I am." She bites her lip. "But it never hurts to have a backup if he doesn't show. And you're way better looking than his profile pic, which probably isn't even of him."

"Sorry, kiddo." I take a sip of beer. "You're not my type."

Her lip protrudes in a pout. Over her shoulder, I notice a guy walk in and scan the crowd. He's tall and thin, with twitchy fingers at his sides. It's not surprising that I don't recognize him; he probably doesn't live in Birchwood Lake. If he's the one meeting Ginger, he likely resides in a nearby town.

Noticing my distraction, Ginger follows my gaze. She and the stranger spot each other simultaneously. I hear her sigh in disappointment, though she doesn't let it show. Instead, she smiles at the man and gives him a little wave.

"Thanks for keeping me company, Wolf," she says. Ginger stands and pulls her skirt down where it's ridden up. The heels of her boots click on the floor as she walks over to my side of the table, bends over, and plants a kiss on my cheek. Across the room, the stranger's expression darkens.

Ginger struts away from my table, putting a sway in her hips. I'm not sure if this little show is for me or the guy she's meeting. I take another swig from the bottle in my hand.

They don't leave right away. Ginger and the man sit at a table just as the waitress delivers my burger. I try to ignore them while I eat. What this young girl does is none of my business. I'm already involved in something I have no business being involved in, and I don't need to add another similar situation into the mix.

Something keeps drawing my eye to their table. It's not Ginger pulling my attention. It's the guy.

Their table is in a shadowy corner, tucked away from everyone else. Do people often take their prostitutes out to dinner? Maybe this is one of those men who wants the girlfriend experience. He wants to pretend that she's actually into him, and that this is a real date.

The man hunches his shoulders. He kind of reminds me of a giant praying mantis with the way he holds his arms, and he can't stop fidgeting. He scratches himself constantly: his arms, his head, the tops of his thighs. Then he reaches out to touch Ginger's hand. Watching him makes the hair rise on the nape of my neck. I can't tell exactly what it is that's throwing a red flag. It could be his shifty behavior or Ginger's youth, but whatever it is, it's making me want to march over there to break up their date and send Ginger home.

I barely notice when my beer and burger are gone. My mind is occupied with thoughts of Ginger and Missy, trying to envision my mostly-silent companion doing what Ginger is doing now. I imagine Missy wearing Ginger's outfit, except with her dyed black hair replaced by a light brown that nearly matches her roots. Sitting beside the tall, thin man, Missy wears a blank expression on her painted face. He tries to make small talk, but hits a brick wall; Missy doesn't engage in idle chatter. Then, they leave together and...

I'm not sure if it's wishful thinking that leads me to assume Missy wouldn't sleep with him, or if it's my intuition. I picture them departing, but I'm uncertain what would happen next if she didn't sleep with him.

When I glance at Ginger's table, the tall man is gone. Ginger sits alone, her elbow resting on the table, chin cupped in the palm of her hand. She looks wistful until she catches my eye and sends me a flirty wave.

There's no food at their table yet, making me wonder if Missy has eaten any of the pizza I brought to the motel. I take a moment to check my phone for missed calls or texts. There's one message from Rebecca, sent over fourteen minutes ago:

"wut happened?? annika dosnt call me 4 notin"

Unsure how to respond, I pocket my phone for now.

On my third beer, I glance at Ginger's table again—it's empty. Immediately, I flag down my waitress and hand her my card. As soon as she brings me my receipt, I throw on my jacket and rush outside.

Night has fully fallen; the air is cold and damp, hinting at rain. I scan the parking lot, searching for a petite girl in revealing clothes. There she is, not far from my truck. I cup my hands around my mouth and shout, "Ginger!"

She startles, teetering on her boot heels before spinning around. Then

Ginger smirks at me. "Hey, Wolf! Did you change your mind?"

I scan the parking lot once more, wondering if I've overlooked anyone. "Where's your friend?"

Ginger rolls her eyes. "Oh, him. He went to the bathroom and never came back. Can you believe it?" She puts her hands on her hips. "Not that I'm super mad about it. He was kinda gross. He kept sucking on his teeth." She shudders. In an instant, Ginger's hand glides up the front of my jacket and plucks at a button. "But since I'm already here, you wanna…"

I catch her wandering hand and gently push her away. "Even if I wanted to, I wouldn't have any way to pay you."

Smirking, Ginger pulls a pen out of her purse and then grabs my hand. The feel of the ballpoint sliding over my palm makes me want to squirm. The pen clicks, and she smiles playfully. "Next time, I'll give you a discount just for not being skeezy."

Tossing her hair over her shoulder, she walks to her car like she's a model on a runway. I look down at my hand. In neat handwriting is a phone number.

Maybe it's because I'm a little drunk, but something propels me back inside the restaurant. I stand in the warm entryway until I see the waitress who I think is in charge of Ginger's section.

"Excuse me?"

Between the customers and the TV, it's so loud that she doesn't hear me right away. I have to approach her and repeat myself two more times before she pauses to look at me.

"Yes, can I help you?"

"Do you remember the man who was sitting at that table?" I point to the dark corner. It's nearly imperceptible the way her eyes dart back and forth while she searches her memory.

"Um … yes. Tall, skinny guy, right?"

"That's the one," I confirm. "Do you know when he left?"

The waitress shakes her head. "No. He and his friend hadn't ordered anything yet, just water. When I came back to take their orders, he was in the restroom. Then they were both gone when I went back a minute ago."

I smile at her gratefully. "That's fine. Thank you."

I move toward the door as if I'm leaving, but once she turns her back, I detour and duck into the men's room.

The air carries a heavy scent of cheap air freshener as I enter the small restroom: two urinals, one stall, and two sinks. The stall door swings open with a creak under pressure. There's no one else here, and no window through which someone could have escaped. I suppose it's possible the guy slipped past Ginger and the waitress, making his way outside. There's no other exit from this room, improbable as it seems that he left the building unnoticed.

I splash cold water on my face to sober up, then head out the door for the final time. The alcohol's warmth is swept away by the biting autumn wind. I drive cautiously, staying five miles under the speed limit. I don't feel drunk, but I'm not sure what my numbers would be if I blew into a breathalyzer. Thankfully, the drive back to the motel is uneventful.

For some reason, I pause outside our room door with my key raised. Listening carefully, I hear faint TV noises from the other side. Pushing the door open, I find Missy on her bed, an empty pizza box beside her. Tension I didn't realize I had dissipates at the sight of her safely engrossed in the television. Her gaze shifts to me standing in the doorway, and she waves— not like Ginger's enticing wave, but the innocent wave of a kid absorbed in TV. I smile and wave back.

"How was your evening?" I ask.

Missy shrugs, stretching her arms above her head.

"Yeah," I say, rubbing the back of my neck. "Mine was the same."

I hang my jacket over a chair and head to the bathroom. I hadn't thought to use the restroom at the restaurant; I was preoccupied then. Now, after a bumpy ride across town, my bladder is fit to burst. I switch on the bathroom light. The ceiling fan sputters at first, then settles into a steady hum. Lifting the toilet seat, I finally relieve the pressure on my bladder.

As I finish up, I glance at the ink on my hand. Have there always been prostitutes around Birchwood Lake? I don't remember seeing anyone like Ginger around these parts when I was a kid. Or perhaps prostitution needed the rise of social media to thrive out here.

I'm about to flush the toilet when I hear a sound: drip, drip, drip. I quickly zip up my jeans and peer into the shower. There's a metal bar meant for hanging washcloths. The other day, it was empty; now, it's draped with wet fabric. Curious, I tug on it.

It's a sweater—a gray V-neck, completely soaked. It lands with a loud smack on the shower floor as I let go. Examining the rack further, I find another piece: a pleated black skirt.

This is the outfit Missy was wearing when I picked her up on the side of the highway—the clothes that went missing. I bring the skirt to my nose; it smells like motel soap. Did Missy try to hand-wash these? Where has she been hiding them, and why didn't she ask me for help?

I carefully hang her skirt and sweater back on the rack. She probably didn't want to feel like a burden. I'll make sure to take her to the laundromat in town tomorrow.

7

This Is the Way We Brush Our Teeth

What did you really look like? In my mind's eye, I remember you perfectly, but whenever I try to describe you to someone else, it's always slightly off. I once went as far as hiring a police sketch artist. I described your porcelain-doll skin, your placid hazel eyes, your dyed black hair with brown roots. It never quite came out right, no matter who I spoke to.

It didn't occur to me until months later that you had somehow warned me about this. That not everyone saw you the way I did. Maybe children and babies didn't see a fifteen-year-old girl, which might explain why you made them cry. It wasn't until I tried to tell Rebecca what you looked like that I began to doubt myself. Was that truly how you appeared, or just a teenage façade you wore? If you were in front of me now, that's one of the questions I would ask you.

I often think back to that moment at the rest stop, where you were twirling in circles, smiling, while a cloud of blackbirds soared overhead. I slow down and recall that memory frame by frame. I catch a glimpse of a different teenage girl, not the one I knew, but one I still recognized. Was it all in my head? Was I projecting that image onto you, or were you playing mind games with me?

I don't hate you. Remember I said that? I hope you're dead, but I don't hate you. It doesn't make sense, I know.

I feel guilty for mocking those who claim to have witnessed UFOs or been abducted by aliens. An experience like that changes how they perceive everything, and people often don't believe them. They can't just pretend it didn't happen and go back

63

to their old lives. That's something most people fail to grasp—something I didn't understand before. I can't return to the life I had because that world doesn't exist anymore.

It's like I'm in a dark room. It's pitch black, the kind of black that makes it impossible to see my hand in front of my face. Then suddenly, for a fraction of a second, the lights come on. In that brief moment, I spot a mountain lion on the opposite side of the room. Then the lights go out again. I'm back in the same darkness that surrounded me before, except now I know there's a predator in the room with me. No one else saw the mountain lion, so they don't believe me. They call me crazy, and eventually, they want me to stop talking about it. But I can't act like everything's normal when I'm wondering when the mountain lion will strike.

I thought I was alone in the dark, but now there's doubt.

***

I wake up early in the morning—or at least, I think I'm awake. There's a hazy film distorting my vision, remnants of sleep or perhaps a dream. My eyes roll, struggling to focus.

The TV screen is dark, curtains drawn shut against moonlight. Finally, I manage to lock my swimming vision onto the red numbers of the clock: 3:24 a.m. Why am I awake? There was enough alcohol in my system to knock me out until sunrise.

I grope for the lamp but fail to find it. If something woke me, I should make sure everything's all right. I should check on Missy.

Her bed is empty, blankets undisturbed. The bathroom light is already on, flooding the carpet with artificial brightness. The ceiling fan hums softly, door ajar. What's she doing in there?

I stumble as I roll out of bed. The room spins, and I clutch at the nightstand. I'm not usually this disoriented waking up at night. I feel more intoxicated now than when the alcohol was fresh. Slowly, I navigate, keeping a hand on the bed, then the wall, as I make my way to the bathroom.

I've never suffered from motion sickness—never on boats, long car rides, or amusement park rides. There were times in my youth I overindulged and paid for it later, but tonight, I know I'm not that drunk. The floor tilts, threatening my stomach's contents.

Reaching the bathroom, I clench my teeth. If I open my mouth, I'll surely expel chunks of half-digested dinner. The bright lights above the toilet and shower blind me, draining color from the room.

Missy kneels in front of the shower, water running, curtain half-closed to contain the splashes. She's without her green hoodie, bare arm under the spray. I grip the door frame to steady myself, taking shaky steps closer. My eyes throb against the assault of light, black spots dancing momentarily. Missy doesn't notice me until I stumble over my heel, grabbing desperately for the towel rack above.

Her limp black hair sways as she turns her head to look at me. I intend to ask what she's doing, but the threat of vomiting halts me. Mouth shut tight, I peer around the shower curtain, fighting vertigo. Initially, I assume she must be washing clothes again. Perhaps I should reassure her about the laundromat in town and offer to help properly clean her clothes in the morning.

But she's not washing clothes.

Her gray sweater and black skirt are gone without a trace, not even her green hoodie in sight. Something lies on the shower floor, definitely not fabric. If she's not washing clothes, why use the shower when there's a sink nearby? Before I can get a clear view, Missy stands abruptly, the room spinning again. It's overwhelming.

I drop to my knees, lifting the toilet lid and burying my head. I retch until there's nothing left. I haven't thrown up in years, not since the last stomach bug. Exhausted, I rest my forehead on the rim, the stench gagging me. Eyes squeezed shut, I fumble for the handle and flush. The taste lingers, rancid. I should find my toothbrush but fear the movement might split my skull open.

Cool fingers on my neck startle me, a memory of fever's sensitivity. Missy pulls me away from the toilet—how she moves me, I don't know. She guides me gently to the floor.

The shower still runs, its sound and stray droplets reaching me. Missy pulls back the curtain, turning off the water. I strain to look—mud traces are visible around her heels. Just before the curtain closes, I see it. Something on the shower floor, multiple tiny off-white objects. That's why she chose the shower over the sink. Those sinks have wider drains; the small white things might have vanished. Squinting, I try to focus. Are those ... molars?

The curtain rings slide shut, blocking my view with a wavering white wall. Head pounding, stomach churning, I watch numbly as Missy steps over me, lights still blazing, the fan humming. Despite the harsh brightness, I finally succumb to sleep.

* * *

I attribute last night to food poisoning. It wasn't severe, as I feel fine just six hours later. Still, it's been ages since I felt that awful. I've never hallucinated with food poisoning or a fever, yet there are no teeth in the shower when I wake on the bathroom floor. Missy's bed shows signs of use, sheets tossed about as if she had trouble sleeping.

The only evidence supporting what I saw is the absence of her clothes. Her sweater and skirt don't reappear in the shower; they're simply gone. In the end, the mystery of appearing and vanishing clothes ranks low on my list. I'll tackle that if I ever solve any of the other puzzles.

I take Missy into town, first for breakfast, then to buy clothes that fit her better than those sweatpants she's worn the past two days. I'd offer to lend her something, but nothing of mine would come close to fitting her.

Entering the coffee shop, I don't feel nauseous, but I'm jittery. I opt for a light breakfast: hot apple cider and an apple turnover for Missy, coffee with cream for myself. We settle at a table in the back near a window overlooking the coffee shop's garden and bench swing.

Missy nibbles at the turnover.

"Did I wake you when I got sick last night?" I ask, sipping my coffee. She shakes her head. "Good."

I must have been seriously out of it to think I saw her in the bathroom. She doesn't show any signs of a rough night—no dark circles, no yawning.

"I think it was food poisoning," I say. "Nothing contagious."

I stretch, easing kinks from my back. A night on the bathroom floor reminds me that I can't sleep on hard surfaces now that I'm past my twenties. I glance up to find Missy gazing outside. Carefully, so I don't strain my neck, I follow her gaze to two girls in the garden, around twelve or thirteen. Not much grows this time of year, but the girls seem fascinated by the swing. I consider suggesting Missy join them, but she looks older than them. A few years make little difference to adults, but to kids, it's vast.

Plus, I sense Missy isn't the social type.

"Do I remind you of your daughter?"

I almost drop my coffee mug—a real ceramic one, not paper—before readjusting my grip just in time. "What was that?" My reply sounds more demanding than questioning. She casually sips her cider.

"Do I remind you of your daughter?" she repeats, setting her cup down and folding her hands. Unconsciously, I touch the albatross charm on my wrist. My heart races, desperate to escape. Every part of me pulses, and my chest tightens as I struggle to breathe. Missy remains calm.

"I heard you," I snap. "What makes you think I have a daughter?"

She toys with her turnover, smearing icing on the plate. "You call me kiddo or Missy," she says. "Not what you'd call a partner. More like a little sister or daughter."

"How very Sherlockian," I mutter. I hadn't considered she would make that connection. Calling her kiddo was automatic. "Kiddo" and "Missy" are childish terms of endearment. But she doesn't know I use them for all kids in my life. I call my nephew kiddo, but she didn't ask if she reminds me of Jeffrey.

I smirk and shake my head. "Missy, you don't remind me of anyone."

"Then why are you helping me?"

"Maybe I'm just a decent human being."

Her lips twitch, reminiscent of the beach. "Decent would mean not leaving me alone on the highway at night. Buying me food and clothes, paying for a second bed—that says something else."

Annoyed now, I cross my arms over my chest. "Oh yeah? Well, I tried handing you over to the cops, but you made that impossible."

"If you didn't want me back in your truck," she replies, "then I wouldn't have gotten back in your truck. If you didn't already want to help me, then you wouldn't have."

I swallow, careful not to choke on my tongue. "Maybe I helped you," I say, "because I know how your parents must be feeling right now."

She smiles a little, though it doesn't reach her eyes, then picks up her hot cider again. Missy returns to staring out the window, signaling the end of our conversation. Her satisfaction with this conclusion contrasts sharply with my own.

Next, we head to a clothing store. I follow her around as she runs her fingers over racks of clothes without showing any interest in them. There are other stores in town we could try, but this one is the most affordable. I won't pressure her if she doesn't find anything she likes here, but finding something that won't burn a hole in my wallet would be ideal.

Fifteen minutes into our wandering, I start to wonder whether she can't find anything she likes or simply doesn't know what she wants. Last time she needed new clothes, I chose them without consulting her. We were rushed then, prioritizing function over style. Is she expecting me to take charge again?

An employee approaches and asks if she can help us. Missy doesn't respond. "We're fine for now," I tell the woman. "Thanks, though."

After she leaves, I place a hand on Missy's shoulder. "How about we find you a pair of pants that fit and don't have a drawstring?"

I guide her to the jeans shelves and sift through sizes. It's been so long since I shopped for women's clothes that I forgot how confusing the sizes are. Their jeans don't list waist sizes in inches—just numbers like four, eight, or twelve. To add to the confusion, sometimes the numbers are even, sometimes odd. I have no idea what these numbers mean. Rebecca only asked me to buy jeans for her once before she realized how clueless I am about it.

Glancing at Missy, I try to estimate if she and Rebecca wear similar sizes around the waist. Missy's hips aren't as pronounced, and she's a bit shorter.

Choosing two different styles of jeans, I grab multiple sizes of each. Next, I lead Missy to shelves of T-shirts and racks of long-sleeved shirts—plain designs, solid colors for the long-sleeved shirts, and swirly flowers and leaves for the T-shirts. I gesture to them.

"Any preference?"

Missy raises her eyebrows, looking between me and the shirts. Mimicking my approach with the jeans, she grabs one of each style. I'm not sure if she chooses sizes she thinks will fit or just the first sizes she touches. It doesn't matter much; she's petite enough that the shirts should fit. It's just odd. It seems like she doesn't know how to shop for clothes. What teenager doesn't know the basics of shopping?

I lead her to the fitting rooms. "Try these on and step out so we can see how they fit."

Missy disappears into the first stall while I take a seat on the bench. Leaning my head back against the wall, I close my eyes. This way, I can pretend I've been dragged out to shop for toys instead of clothes. I imagine the girl with me eagerly running through the store, showing me everything she likes. With this other girl, I wouldn't have to pull teeth to get her opinion.

Suddenly, my mind flashes back to the motel bathroom. I'm on the floor, looking between Missy's ankles at the molars in the shower. This time, there are more teeth—incisors and cuspids. The tiles are pink as blood mixes with water and trickles down the drain.

My eyes snap open. Better not to linger on sick-induced nightmares.

The stall door creaks, and Missy steps out. She's dressed in a pair of bootcut jeans and a dark purple T-shirt. It's the first time I've seen her in anything formfitting, making it very obvious now that she isn't wearing a bra.

Quickly, I stand up and look anywhere except at Missy. "Uh, wait here a minute."

If women's pant sizes mildly confuse me, then I know I don't have a prayer of decoding bra sizes. Sports bras seem like the best option. I grab a small black one off the rack. It strikes me that she might not have underwear either. Definitely no *spare* underwear, so she'll need another pair anyway. I find a pack of plain cotton panties, and as a last-minute thought, I pick up a package of socks as well. Then I hurry back to the changing rooms.

I'm fairly confident the underwear and socks will fit her, so the only thing she really needs to try on is the sports bra. I thrust it at Missy when I duck back into the alcove.

"Here, put this on underneath your shirt."

She briefly examines the bra. I sit down on the bench and take a deep breath. I'm ridiculously thankful the helpful sales lady didn't try to assist me in picking out these items.

The next time Missy emerges from the stall, I can vaguely see the lines of the sports bra under another T-shirt. She's wearing a dark blue, long-sleeved shirt and another pair of jeans. Everything appears to fit her just fine; nothing is noticeably too tight or loose.

"What do you think?"

There are three full-length mirrors in the alcove, tilted toward the customer so they can see their outfit from different angles. Missy ignores them and faces me with an expectant look. I chuckle and shake my head.

"Don't look at me, weirdo. Look in the mirror."

I stand and put my hands on her shoulders, gently coaxing her to face the three mirrors. She studies her reflection. Missy doesn't seem pleased or critical. It's more like she is looking at something she doesn't understand, similar to how I must look every time I peek under the hood of my truck. It's hard to form an opinion when I don't fully grasp what I'm seeing.

"You don't care about this at all," I surmise.

She meets my gaze in the mirror and raises one eyebrow. For some reason, this strikes my funny bone. Barking out a laugh, I release her shoulders.

"Okay. We'll get these and be done. Why don't you wear that up to the register?"

After we leave the shop, I drive us to the laundromat. Missy isn't the only one who could stand to wash her clothes. I am well aware of the state of my dirty laundry by the end of the week; it's best not to let it stew in my bag for too long. The whole time we're at the laundromat, I keep thinking that she must be bored to death. But there's never a word, or even a look, of complaint from her. In fact, she seems fascinated by the swirling water inside the washing machines.

It's only when I take her to dinner that I realize how quickly the day has flown by. Having someone else to do these mundane tasks with makes a difference. If it were just me going clothes shopping and doing laundry, the morning and afternoon would have dragged. It's funny that someone so quiet can be engaging company. Now that I know she can understand me and respond when she wants, I feel less like I'm talking to myself.

We return to the motel after dinner. I don't know about Missy, but I'm beat. I don't get out of the truck right away once I've parked. Neither does Missy. Something I've realized in recent years is that you don't have to be physically alone to be lonely. I've been surrounded by friends and family and still felt lonely. I've attended church, concerts, had someone sleep next to me all night, and still felt lonely.

But today, I didn't feel lonely. Not once. Right now, someone else is lonely without Missy.

"Did you run away from home?" I ask softly. "Be honest."

Missy shakes her head. I think back to the sweater and skirt that looked like a uniform.

"Did you run away from school?"

Again, Missy shakes her head.

"Are you going home?" I ask, thinking perhaps she ran away before and now she's on her way back, but she shakes her head. "Then where are you going?"

My voice is rougher than I intend. Frustration has my fingers curling tighter around the steering wheel.

"Listen." I sigh and rub a hand over my jaw. "I like your company. I don't mind looking after you, but you gotta understand how this looks for me. I picked up a kid on the side of the road and didn't tell anybody? Cops are gonna think I took you. Even Carson will believe that. He'll think I had a nervous breakdown, that I didn't mean any harm, but he'll still arrest me. Probably have me committed too."

"You're worried someone is looking for me."

I realize only now how expressive she's been today. It's hard to believe that just two days ago, she had as much life in her face as a mannequin. Her features are slack now, as if she hasn't smiled, pursed her lips, or arched her brow at me all afternoon. Her glassy eyes are fixed straight ahead through the windshield. She doesn't blink, doesn't fidget.

"No one is looking for me."

For the rest of the evening, neither of us speaks. I suspect I've exhausted all her words for today. As for me, I'm simply tired. But what she said bothers me. She spoke without hesitation, with unwavering conviction. How lonely it must be to genuinely believe that no one is looking for her.

8

Eat Off His Head

T he most frightening nightmare that still haunts me is the one about the teeth.

The difference between that dream and the one with the shadow driver nags at me. The one with the mysterious driver is crystal clear in my mind. I'm not usually one of those people who relives memories in their dreams. I have nonsense dreams or I dream about fantasies. I can't tell you how many times I've dreamed about the doorbell ringing and looking through the window to see blue eyes gazing back at me from the front steps, golden brown hair cascading from her head, and freckles dotting her smiling face. That dream has a hazy quality, as most dreams do. But my dream about the shadowy driver? It's like I'm watching it in high resolution. It feels real.

On the other hand, the nightmare about the teeth is definitely a memory. Either a memory of something I actually saw or a memory of a hallucination. Whether the event really took place is beside the point. The point is that the dream is based on recall. You'd think I would have a clear image of those teeth in the shower, but I swear my nightmare about the teeth is even fuzzier than normal dreams.

Have you ever played that memory game where a bunch of images flash by on a screen, and then you have to recite as many as you can in the order you saw them? That's how I feel when I dream about the teeth. And I always lose that game.

You want to hear another theory of mine? I think the dreams were the only times I saw the truth about you. The more time that passes, the more certain I become that

73

you actually were washing teeth in the shower—whose teeth, I can't say. Maybe they belonged to the thin, fidgety man at the Blue Fox. You did something to put me in a deep sleep, but somehow I woke up and interrupted you. It wasn't food poisoning, and I wasn't drunk. I believe you were also the shadow driving my truck. God knows I wasn't in charge of the situation.

I spent most of our time together looking the other way whenever you did something strange. Because that's what people do, isn't it? We bend over backwards to explain anything that doesn't neatly fit into our reality. I explained away seeing those teeth in the shower as a weird side effect of food poisoning. I wish that was where it ended. I wish you had been better at hiding things from me.

* * *

The next day, I decide to show Missy where I used to live. It's nice outside, and I'm sick of being in the truck, so I suggest we walk. As usual, she passively complies. I'll have to watch for signs of weariness or sore feet, since I'm sure she won't say anything. She wears a pair of jeans that we bought yesterday, along with a green, long-sleeved shirt. Before we leave the motel, she tries to stuff her bare feet into her black shoes. She gives me a blank look when I show her the socks I bought for her, but after a minute, she puts them on.

We exit our room and walk down the street toward the beach. Today, we skirt around it, avoiding the sand but not the distinct fishy smell. On the other side of the beach is Birchwood's tiny library. This isn't a library to visit if you're searching for something specific. Most people go to this library just to browse and see what they find. The building consists of only one room. The librarian's desk is situated next to the front door. Three walls are lined floor to ceiling with books, and the aisles are astonishingly narrow to fit as many shelves as possible.

"A short detour can't hurt," I suggest.

Mr. Jacobs was the head librarian when I was a kid. The man's rosy cheeks reminded me of Santa Claus. He was a hefty guy who somehow maneuvered the aisles of the miniature library expertly. It was like watching a bull gracefully prance through a china shop. When Missy and I enter the building, I immediately feel like I'm twelve years old again. I used to be convinced that this place was magical.

My head turns to the right, and there he is, just as comically large as in my memory. Mr. Jacobs dwarfs the librarian's desk. He's not just wide around the middle; he's also a giant. He's taller than me, and I didn't exactly grow up to be a hobbit. His hair and beard are whiter than freshly fallen snow, the only aspect of his appearance that time has changed. He still wears flannel shirts that are a little too small for him, the black buttons strained, making a herculean effort to keep the man contained. He looks up as the screen door bangs shut behind us.

"Morning!" His doughy face parts and stretches so we can see his huge smile beneath his bushy beard. "How can I help you folks?"

It's impossible not to smile back at Mr. Jacobs. His good humor is contagious, and he sounds like Goofy when he chuckles. No matter how bad I felt in the past, Mr. Jacobs could always get a smile out of me. He hasn't lost his touch.

I extend my hand to him. "Hi, Mr. Jacobs. I don't know if you remember me, but I used to live in Birchwood Lake."

He shakes my hand and pulls me closer to get a better look at my face. As soon as he releases me, he takes a pair of bifocals from the desk and peers through them.

"You look familiar," he says, "but you'll have to forgive me. There are a fair few names I've forgotten over the years. What's yours, young man?"

"Kevin Wolf. My sister and I, along with Carson Goodall, used to come in here all the time."

Mr. Jacobs smacks the palm of his hand on the desk, creating a man-made clap of thunder. "That's right! Mr. Wolf, how are you? How's your sister? Her name is Annika, isn't it?"

"Yeah, that's her." I step back as Mr. Jacobs hoists himself out of his chair and comes around the desk. The piece of furniture shakes, and the knickknacks on it wobble. "She's, uh, she's doing all right."

He jovially pats my shoulder. My knees buckle just a bit, but I keep my balance and clear my throat.

"I actually come back to Birchwood every year, but I don't usually make a stop at the library."

Mr. Jacobs scratches his beard. "But I believe I recall you coming in here several years ago. You had a young lady with you?"

Honestly, I'm surprised he remembers that. Back in the day, when Rebecca and I were still together, we didn't have the time to stay in Birchwood Lake for a whole week. We would come up here for the Fall Festival, and the next we'd leave for home. Not much time for sightseeing. We only came here again to visit my parents for Christmas, and the library is closed for major holidays. One year, though, I told Rebecca the story about Carson finding a crawlspace in the library. He told Annika that there was a skeleton hidden in there. By the time he finally convinced my sister to look in the crawlspace, he had slipped a motion-activated toy right inside the opening. It was one of those doohickeys you buy around Halloween; when someone walks past it, a speaker lets loose a wild cackle. Annika gave Carson a black eye for that joke.

After hearing the story, Rebecca wanted to go to the library and see if we could find the crawlspace. We found it, but it looked like someone had nailed a piece of plywood over the opening. Mr. Jacobs wasn't there when we stopped by. A woman was at the desk, but we did see him briefly on our way out. We were late meeting my parents for lunch, so we were literally running out of the library when Mr. Jacobs was arriving. I waved to him and said hello, but that was it.

"Yep," I say, trying to dredge up a smile that isn't melancholy. "That was me and my girlfriend at the time."

"I see. Well, I'm glad I get to talk to you this time, son." He shifts his massive body to the side and peers around me. "And who is this young lady?"

Craning my neck to look over my shoulder, I'm startled to find Missy's nose is nearly touching my jacket. When did she creep so close to me? Lifting my arm, I lay my palm on the crown of her head.

"This is my niece Missy."

Too late, I realize that the niece story might be difficult to sell to someone who has met my sister. Missy doesn't resemble Annika at all. My sister and I look a lot alike. Annika has light brown hair that's straight as wheat stalks and gunmetal blue eyes that she always wished were green. In short, she looks very Scandinavian. Missy has lighter skin than either me or Annika. Even without the black hair dye, I can tell by her roots that she would have darker hair than either of us. There's also nothing about her facial features that makes Missy look like a member of the Wolf family.

Mr. Jacobs doesn't call my bluff. He smiles down at her and holds out his hand. "Nice to meet you, Missy. I'm Richard Jacobs, the head librarian here."

Missy stares at his hand and doesn't move an inch, remaining hidden behind me. Mr. Jacobs doesn't make a big deal out of it. He claps, sending a cloud of dust swirling through the air.

"So, did you come by just to reminisce, or are you looking for an adventure?"

I'm drowning in nostalgia now. Mr. Jacobs always called books adventures. That's what got me to enjoy reading. Without waiting for an answer, the librarian scoots past me and Missy, moving down the main aisle, which is only slightly wider than the others. He ducks between two shelves, shuffling sideways at a quick pace. The way he maneuvers around the cramped library reminds me of a sidewinder snake. It looks so odd that I can't take my eyes off him.

"What sort of adventures do you like, Missy?" His booming voice fills the tiny building, nearly shaking the rafters. "Do you like stories about outer space or about young people at boarding schools? How about stories about pirates or medieval fantasy worlds? Or do you prefer your adventures to be set in a dystopian future?"

Missy's fingers clench into a fist twisted in my jacket. Is she afraid of Mr. Jacobs? The man is huge, but his enormous stature isn't intimidating. He's a giant teddy bear lumbering around this itty-bitty library. She wasn't afraid of me when we met at night on a lonely highway—and I've seen myself. I don't look nearly as affable as Mr. Jacobs. I look like the kind of guy who might pick up hitchhikers and make them disappear. And yet, she was perfectly fine getting into my truck. Now that she's faced with the cousin of Jolly Old Saint Nick, she wants to use me as a human shield.

I walk down the narrow passage, following Mr. Jacobs and dragging Missy behind me. She's really digging her heels into the floor. I can hear the treads of her shoes squeaking as they slide.

Mr. Jacobs is down the third row looking through books at lightning speed. He pulls two off the shelf, glances at the backs of them, nods, and stacks them on a cart parked on the other end of the aisle.

"Sorry," I say, "Missy's a little shy. It's nothing personal. She barely talks to *me*."

"No offense taken, Mr. Wolf," the man laughs. "I've met a wide variety of children over the years. It takes a great deal more to offend me these days." Placing one hand on the cart, he sucks in his gut enough for Missy to see the books he plucked off the shelf. The aisle is too narrow for Mr. Jacobs to turn around completely. "Well, Missy, if you decide you'd like something to read while you're in town, these are a few of my favorites for young adult fiction."

Mr. Jacobs shoos us out of the way so that he can shimmy into the main aisle.

"What about you, Mr. Wolf?"

It's a strange time to remember this, but hearing Mr. Jacobs say it now, I think he might have been the one who got everybody else to start calling me by my last name. Carson heard the librarian call me Mr. Wolf and thought it sounded so cool. He started barking and howling at me whenever we saw each other; he tried doing the same to Annika, but she gave him another shiner to match the first one.

"I'm not sure I'll have time to read while I'm here," I tell him. "I was just going to show Missy the house where I grew up. We were passing by the library, and I thought I'd see if you still worked here."

Mr. Jacobs chuckles that cartoonish laugh of his. Behind me, I feel Missy release her hold on my jacket. She is merely a flash of movement as she slips between bookshelves and disappears farther into the library.

"Oh, you know me," says Mr. Jacobs. "I've been here so long, they'll probably bury me out back after I die. But tell me more about you. What have you been up to all these years?"

We spend the next ten minutes talking about my work and how Birchwood Lake has changed over time. The entire time, Missy remains hidden. I briefly wonder if she has discovered the boarded-up crawlspace at the back of the building. I bring up the crawlspace incident with Annika and Carson and get rewarded with more infectious laughter. It's apparently one of Mr. Jacobs' favorite stories to retell. He said he had to cover the crawlspace because he worried that some kid would get the brilliant idea to squeeze into the opening and get themselves stuck.

Occasionally, I notice the librarian's attention wander. His deep-set eyes slide casually to the right before coming back to me. Nothing outlandish, except Mr. Jacobs is not the inattentive sort.

Eventually, I decide it's time to move on, though I make a mental note to come by before I leave town. I'm about to call out to Missy when I realize that she has sidled up to me again. "There you are." I pat her head. "I was just about to ask if you were ready to leave."

Missy doesn't waste any time. The suggestion has barely left my mouth when she zips past the front desk and out the door. I guess I have my answer. Mr. Jacobs' jovial attitude, which has been warmly lighting the library, fades now that the two of us are alone together. Thinking that we have managed to offend him, despite what he claimed earlier, I'm about to apologize. However, the older man speaks first.

"That young lady isn't your niece, is she."

He doesn't pose it as a question, though he doesn't sound like he's condemning me either. Mr. Jacobs is still smiling, but his smile is diminished. More sorrowful. I don't know what to tell him.

"It's…" I'm about to say it's a long story, only it isn't. It's actually a very short story. I settle for, "It's complicated."

The skin around Mr. Jacobs' eyes wrinkles pleasantly, even though his smile remains sad. "I had a feeling it was. Just do me a favor, Mr. Wolf." The man rests a massive hand on my shoulder. "Be careful."

I clear my throat before speaking. "Yes, sir."

"Good." He pats my shoulder and returns to the desk. "Don't be a stranger. Be sure to say goodbye to me before you set off for home."

I promise that I will and then make my way to the front of the building. As I'm pushing the door open, I glance over my shoulder.

Mr. Jacobs is seated at the desk, no longer smiling at all. He frowns at the opposite wall as he wrings his hands.

* * *

I feel bad that Missy didn't enjoy our trip to the library, especially since she seemed distressed. As we walk past the bakery, I pop in and buy us both treats: a maple-bacon donut for me and a frosted, jelly-filled donut for Missy. She actually points to the one she wants, which is more input than I usually get from her when it comes to food. The bell clinks against the door as we exit.

A cluster of crows on the sidewalk caw and scatter, making way for us. Inhaling the sweet scent of autumn, I gaze up at the colors of the leaves as we walk. The sun is deigning to show its face today, giving the town a markedly less dreary appearance and showcasing all the vibrant hues of the trees. The cracked, weathered sidewalk brings me back to the days when I had to perform all kinds of tricky moves on my skateboard to avoid catching a wheel on fallen acorns.

Birchwood Lake is the sort of town that helps you raise a family. Reminiscing over the past few days, I am amazed at how many families besides my own nurtured me as a kid. There was Carson's family, Mr. Jacobs, and just about every adult on my street. They all gave me a place to hang out after school and kept me out of too much trouble. I don't regret moving out of state when I turned eighteen—if I hadn't, I might not have met Rebecca, and I wouldn't trade my time with her for anything—but I wish I had come back before my life went sideways.

It seems too late to come home now. My own family is broken, and the town has moved on without me. The only piece of my childhood that I have left is the Fall Festival.

I think about where Missy is from. I don't know of any boarding schools in the state, so I assume she's relatively local. If her sweater and skirt are part of a uniform, then it's likely a private school, which suggests either a wealthy family or a girl on a scholarship.

I don't know who she is, where she came from, or where she's going. I don't know if she grew up in a town like Birchwood Lake or if she's from a sprawling city. I don't know if Birchwood is the kind of place she's looking for or if her horizons extend farther than this.

I try to imagine Missy being friends with a little blue-eyed girl who likes to tie ribbons in her long, golden hair. I can't picture it, though. I can't picture Missy being friends with anyone. I can't see Missy with a family or in a classroom. She's so solitary that trying to picture her with imaginary peers feels wrong. The way she acts and speaks makes her seem like she's always been alone—no friends, no family. No one is looking for her.

Something tugs at the paper bag clutched in my hand. Looking down, I see Missy plucking at the bag from the bakery. I loosen my grip, allowing her to open it and place her half-eaten donut inside. With her hands free, Missy links her arm with mine. I search her face. She smiles demurely, her hazel eyes turned toward the sky. Following her gaze, I see the branches overhead are filled with blackbirds. A couple of them caw as we pass beneath them.

A squirrel scampers directly across our path. The little guy quickens his stride and screeches at us before scurrying up a tree. Missy's smile vanishes faster than a popped balloon. A cold, placid expression covers her face. She stares at the squirrel until the animal is out of sight. By the time we reach the end of the block, I can still hear the squirrel yelling at us.

We round the corner, and Missy's arm falls from the crease of my elbow. It dangles limply at her side. Her face is blank. Anxiety rises from somewhere deep inside me; it makes me want to say something to make her laugh or confuse her—anything to get a human reaction. It takes great effort to smother that impulse and soothe my nerves some other way. In the few minutes that it takes us to reach my old house, I feel a little better. Missy, on the other hand, is still withdrawn.

Whoever bought my parents' home hasn't changed much. It still looks kind of like a barn with pale blue siding and stonework closer to the ground. The only notable difference is the flowers lining the sidewalk. Neither of my parents had a green thumb, plus Annika and I would have trampled any flowers they planted. I can't count the number of times I heard, "Get out of my lilac bushes, Kevin!" as I cut through the elderly Mrs. Henderson's backyard.

"Here it is," I say to Missy. "This is the house I grew up in." I glance at her from the corner of my eye and see her blank expression soften. Bending down, Missy gently strokes the petals of an orange snapdragon. "Do you have roots planted somewhere?" I ask her. "Someplace to go back to?"

She squeezes the base of the snapdragon to make the flower's mouth pop open. "I'm not a tree," she says. "I don't have roots."

I roll my eyes. "I know, kid. I was just asking if you have a place that makes you feel at home. The roots are a metaphor."

She smiles faintly. "So is the tree."

Missy looks playful again, but it's at my expense. Not that I mind; I just wish I could make more sense out of her words. Folding my arms, I heave a sigh.

"I'm never going to understand you, am I?"

Missy shakes her head. "No, I'm not a tree."

"And the tree is a metaphor."

She nods.

"Okay. Well, I think I'm done trying to wrap my brain around you. So far, it's only given me a headache."

I take in the front of the house one last time. It would be fun to ring the bell and see if anyone is home, but whoever the current owners are, I'm probably a stranger to them. And Missy is definitely a stranger. Seeing it from the outside will have to be enough.

All of a sudden, Missy takes off sprinting down the sidewalk in the direction we came from. I stand frozen for a moment. Why is she running? There are no cars driving up the street, no pedestrians except the two of us, and nothing moving except leaves blown by the wind.

I run after her.

I gain some ground once we're a block away from my old house. She isn't running anymore. Now, Missy stands under an oak tree and stares down at something on the sidewalk. In my younger years, sprinting around the block wouldn't even wind me. These days, I'm closer to forty than I am to thirty. I'm breathing heavily, and something in the region of my knee creaks and twinges.

"Hey," I say, then pause to gulp down air. "What gives?"

I join Missy and look down at the decapitated body of a squirrel. Gulping, I take a step away from the carcass.

"What the hell did that?" I mutter. "I don't remember that being there when we first walked by."

Looking left then right, I don't see the head anywhere. It could have been eaten. I had a cat when I was a kid, and it always ate the heads first whenever it killed rabbits or mice.

Missy's body is stiff when I place a hand on her elbow.

"Come on, kiddo. Let's go."

***

She never finishes her donut. For most of the day, I forget about the bakery paper bag sitting untouched on the table in our motel room. It's not until that night, while Missy is in the bathroom preparing for bed, that I remember there's still half a jelly-filled donut inside the bag.

The donut juice has left a greasy stain on the white paper, and some of the jelly filling must have leaked because the damp spot is tinged red. There's no way she wants to eat that after it's been sitting here for hours.

I swing my legs over the side of the bed and pad across the bare carpet. Initially, I plan to throw the bag away, but as I reach for it, a quiet but insistent voice in the back of my head speaks up. *Open the bag,* it says.

Unexpected trepidation fills me. I glance at the closed bathroom door. With unsteady hands, I carefully uncurl the top of the paper bag.

A foul smell rises to greet me, and I jerk back, gagging. Taking a deep breath through my mouth this time, I approach the bag again. Inside, the white frosting on the pastry has melted and become runny. Rusty red filling has spilled from Missy's bite marks. The color and consistency of the filling seem odd—not like jelly, which would still be shiny and sticky hours later. This filling is dull and dry, resembling old hamburger meat. It smells a little like that too, only worse.

I pull the bag open wider.

That's definitely not jelly filling. It's chunky and brownish-red. I tilt the bag closer to the light to get a better look. Is that … a tongue?

Out of nowhere, a dizzy spell hits me. My eyes lose focus on the contents of the bag. It feels like the night I woke up with food poisoning, minus the nausea. I drop the bag and grab the edge of the table for balance. Exhaustion wraps around me like a boa constrictor. Somehow, I manage to stumble back to bed. As soon as my body is horizontal, sleep wins the battle.

9

A Lady All Skin and Bone

I'm pleased to say that I wasn't blind to you after the donut incident. Well, maybe "pleased" isn't the right word. Let's put it this way: I would have been even more ashamed of my obliviousness if I had ignored discovering a donut filled with a human tongue. Since you left, I've been curious. Why were you afraid of Mr. Jacobs? You certainly didn't seem frightened of him the next time the two of you met. And what did he see in you that made him warn me to be careful? Everyone else who came into contact with you just felt uneasy and didn't really know why.

Whatever you did to dull my instincts, I think you did the same thing to lull me to sleep and confuse me whenever I saw something you didn't intend for me to see. But there was only so much you could do to conceal your clandestine activities. The longer you stayed with me, the harder it became to keep secrets.

"If I didn't already want to help you, then I wouldn't have." That's what you said. I've had a while to think about that, and here's what I believe you meant: the only power you had over me was the power I gave you. If I didn't already want to help you, then you couldn't have forced me to. If I truly wanted to uncover what you were doing, your mind tricks wouldn't have worked on me.

Whatever wrongs you committed, I share the blame for willingly turning a blind eye. If anyone other than you ever reads these letters, I'm sure I'll get a lecture about taking on guilt that isn't rightfully mine. Do you understand how guilt works? I know you recognize emotions and can feign them to a degree, but do you <u>understand</u>

85

them? You once told me that because I was a tree and you weren't, I would never understand you. Well, I think the opposite is true too. You observe other people, but you don't know what it's like to feel the way we do. That is, assuming I'm right about you being inhuman. If I'm not ... well, I guess I'm back to square one.

Do you understand that you've changed me? I'm not talking about a change in behavior. I mean deep inside. I think and see the world differently now.

Because of you.

***

The Fall Festival decorations are going up all over town. Hay bales line Main Street, store owners adorn their display windows with pumpkins, jack-o'-lanterns, and fake spiderwebs, and skeletons, witches, and zombies are visible from every street corner in Birchwood. Despite not appearing like a town that's into Halloween, Birchwood Lake's residents have embraced the autumn spirit over the years.

However, I'm not feeling as festive as everyone else.

The night I thought I saw Missy washing teeth in the shower, I could blame it on possible food poisoning from the Blue Fox. But I have no explanation for the sudden dizziness and fatigue when I saw the tongue spilling out of her half-eaten donut. For the first time since meeting her, I'm wary of Missy—not just about the potential repercussions of taking her off the highway without notifying anyone except Carson. I'm cautious of her and what she might do.

It's perplexing because she's a teenager, a small person I could easily bench press. Without a weapon, how much harm could she do? Yet, I can't ignore the numerous red flags I've noticed. Strange occurrences seem to follow her—disappearing and reappearing clothes, bizarre dreams, teeth, and a severed tongue in her donut. It's all becoming too strange to overlook.

When I drive into town for coffee and breakfast, I leave Missy behind. Lately, she's been spending longer in the bathroom. Most girls her age would be primping and preening, but in our motel room, the mirror is situated away from the toilet and shower, above two sinks. I've never seen her wear makeup, and I'm not even sure if she brushes her hair. I've never been a teenage girl, but I can't think of any other reason she'd be occupied in there if not for using the shower or toilet.

I don't know, and I'm wondering if I should even care.

At the Lakeside Diner, as I pick up my coffee, bacon, and eggs to go, I inadvertently overhear a snippet of conversation mentioning the Blue Fox and that Ginger girl—and I freeze.

At a nearby table sit two men and one woman, all appearing slightly older than me, maybe in their mid-forties. They've finished eating; only crumbs and syrup streaks remain on their plates. Now they're just shooting the breeze, sipping leisurely on their coffees.

"…wish they wouldn't let that harlot through the door." The woman folds her arms and reclines in her chair. "Gives the Blue Fox a bad name, if ya ask me."

"It doesn't make a lick of difference as long as she's not doin' anything illegal on the property," says the man wearing a cap with a camouflage pattern on it. "Ginger and her johns only eat there. She don't even try to drink. Money and services get exchanged somewhere else."

The bearded man next to him snorts and clears a wad of phlegm from his throat. I turn to the stack of Tidbits papers on the partition and pretend to browse through one. The flash of the bearded man's bright orange hunting vest catches my eye as he spits into his napkin.

"I always figured *she'd* end up on a milk carton someday," the bearded guy remarks. "Maybe one of her clients got jealous. Unless the guy has enemies that got nothin' to do with Ginger, then I don't see any other explanation."

"You'd think someone would have seen something," the woman adds. "People don't just disappear into thin air."

I fold the Tidbits I was holding and slip it into my to-go bag. I realize I've been holding my breath, black spots clouding my vision. The sleazy guy who met Ginger at the Blue Fox is missing? I already knew Ginger and the waitress didn't see him leave the restaurant, but now he's officially a missing person?

People don't just vanish.

The woman's words echo in my mind. Such a confident statement. Rebecca and I know better than most that sometimes people do just vanish. They disappear without a trace.

Have you seen a young girl, eight years old? She has light brown hair, and she was wearing...

What was she wearing?

Sometimes, people fall through the cracks.

I get in the truck and set my food on the vacant passenger seat. For a minute, I sit there doing nothing. Returning to Birchwood Lake for the Fall Festival isn't supposed to be about this—desperately searching a sea of people for one child with ribbons in her hair. Those aren't the memories I want to relive. Memories where I'm falling, waiting to either be saved at the last moment or to hit the ground, but neither happens. I just keep falling and falling and falling.

Returning to Birchwood Lake in autumn is the only time I'm not falling. It's my only respite. I can't lose this one harbor when the rest of the year is open ocean, full of hurricanes and desolate waters with no land in sight. The guy Ginger was with the other night will turn up at some point. He has to.

* * *

Around lunchtime, I take Missy out for food and sightseeing. I avoid mentioning the man who went missing at the Blue Fox—it feels risky. Bringing it up wouldn't align with Mr. Jacobs' warning to be cautious. Besides, I reassure myself, she doesn't know anything about it.

But what if she does? a doubtful voice in my head persists. *Are you afraid she'll think you aren't worth the trouble if you don't act oblivious? What then? We're all afraid of being left in the dark...*

As we wait for our food, a small hand slips into mine. Missy gazes up at me with wide, innocent eyes. Her finger brushes my tattoo, momentarily calming the doubts buzzing in my mind like nagging flies. She leans into my side, audibly sighing through flared nostrils. It's reassuring to feel her knuckle gently touching the albatross on my wrist.

A strange conviction washes over me.

Whoever Missy is, she harbors no ill intentions toward me. The best way I can explain this certainty is by likening her to a tiger in a zoo. As long as there's glass between us, I'm safe—the tiger won't harm me. Similarly, despite all the odd occurrences, I'm convinced I'm not the one in danger. I'm on the safe side of the glass.

Our two orders of Swedish meatballs are set on a tray. Missy trails closely as I carry our lunches to an open table. Seated across from each other, we both have plates of meatballs smothered in gravy, mashed potatoes, and roasted asparagus. Steam rises, enveloping her face in a hazy cloud. She blinks and takes an inquisitive sniff.

"These are the best meatballs you will ever taste," I declare.

Using my fork, I spear a meatball and savor the hot, savory sauce coating my tongue. I close my eyes briefly, reveling in the flavor. Opening them, I check if Missy has tried hers yet. She holds a meatball on her fork, alternating between examining it and looking at me. I briefly wonder if she'll eat it whole like I did, but she doesn't.

Missy sticks her tongue out and pokes the meatball lightly. The pink muscle darts back into her mouth. She blinks rapidly, smacking her lips. She reminds me of a certain round-faced baby who decided to lick soap suds off her hands. My laughter comes out as a snort, and I dig into the mashed potatoes.

The meal is interrupted by my phone vibrating. Annika's name lights up the screen. My initial urge is to decline the call, but that would only result in my sister bombarding my phone with increasingly angry and threatening voicemails and texts. With a sigh, I answer.

"Hey, Annika."

"Hey. So, I can get the rest of the week off work, and Paul will watch the kids. But I can't catch a plane until late tomorrow night or early Wednesday morning."

Taken aback, I sit with my mouth agape for a moment while I try to find words. "Catch a plane?" I repeat. "Annika, what are you talking about?"

"Kev, you're giving Carson and Rebecca the runaround when something is obviously going on. If you're not going to tell me or them what it is, then I'm coming up there to see for myself."

I roll my eyes. Covering the bottom half of the phone with my palm, I whisper to Missy, "Just a second, kiddo. I'll be right back."

I step outside the little restaurant onto the sidewalk. I can envision Annika impatiently crossing her arms as I put the phone back to my ear.

"Everything's fine, Annika. Don't get on a plane."

"Then can you *please* tell me what's going on? Because I got the same line from Carson after you finally called him back. But the first time he called me, he said you claimed to have picked up a phantom hitchhiker and thought you'd found a missing girl. You can see why that might concern me and Rebecca, right?"

"You know, sometimes I hate that you two still talk to each other."

"Well, you should have thought about that before you married one of my coworkers."

A pause follows, long enough for me to think I've safely navigated out of treacherous waters. Annika's surprisingly protective, considering she's the younger sibling. She never needed her big brother to save the day; it's always been little sister to the rescue. That's why I shouldn't have assumed she'd let me off that easy.

"I'm not trying to baby you, Kevin. I just want to know that you're not in the middle of a crisis."

I blow a slow gust of air past my lips. "I'm not in a crisis. And she wasn't a phantom hitchhiker. There was a girl who wandered off when I tried to involve Carson, then showed up again after he left Perkins. I just helped her get where she was going. It's all good now. I don't need you to hop on a plane for an intervention."

A sigh, echoing my own, comes from the other end of the line. "Okay, I'll butt out. But you owe me a visit when you get home! No pretending you're too busy or forgot that I was coming over."

Bullet dodged.

"Yeah, yeah, I promise. I was in the middle of lunch when you called, so I gotta go."

"All right. I'll see you when you get back. Bye, Kev."

"Bye."

Well, that could've gone worse. If I hadn't answered, she might've actually booked a flight. A meeting between Annika and Missy is something I can't imagine. My sister wouldn't understand why Missy is still with me.

Pocketing my phone, I turn to go back inside. The front of this hole-in-the-wall restaurant has one long window spanning its length. From here, I've got a decent view of the table I share with Missy. Our corner is partially cast in shadows, but I can still see her eating meatballs and mashed potatoes. She must have decided she likes the food after all. I start to walk through the entrance when something else catches my eye.

The thing on the end of her fork is covered in the restaurant's special gravy, but it's not a meatball. It's an eyeball. She pops it into her mouth and chews.

My legs are little more than dead weight on my walk back to the table. By the time I arrive, Missy is eating normal Swedish meatballs. I sit down and give her a stern look. At first, she doesn't seem to notice. When she finally does, her eyes widen innocently.

"I'm not someone who daydreams vividly," I tell her. "And I don't have any illnesses that cause me to see or hear things that aren't there."

I want her to understand that I see through her act without making her feel cornered. Breaking eye contact, I resume eating. My food has turned lukewarm. It's things like this that I'm afraid Annika would notice if she met Missy. While I'm willing to sweep almost anything under the rug, my sister has always been much more direct.

"How do you know what's real?"

Missy's voice catches me off guard.

"Well..." It takes me a few seconds to gather my thoughts. "If the majority of people can all see, hear, smell, taste, or touch the same thing, then it's probably real."

"How do you know what *they're* experiencing is real?"

I let my fork clank against my plate instead of setting it down gently. "Because, Missy, we don't live in the Matrix." Then under my breath, I add, "I think I liked it better when you were mute."

Just as I'm about to lift my fork to my mouth, she interrupts again.

"But how do you know?"

I throw my fork down for the second time. Fine, let my food go cold. Meeting Missy's gaze squarely, I rest my arms on the table.

"Are you asking me how I know that I'm not in the Matrix?" She nods. "Because that's a movie. Stuff like that doesn't happen in real life."

"How do you know?"

"Is there an echo in here? I know because I'm thirty-seven years old, kid. Things in sci-fi movies don't happen in real life. If they did, most of the world would've heard about them by now. That's how I know."

"So, you don't know."

"If you're gonna be a brat, then I'm not arguing with you."

With that, I stuff two Swedish meatballs into my mouth. A fleeting smile appears on Missy's face before she returns to finish her food.

* * *

"Don't look at me like that, Missy. It's not that far of a walk."

Missy keeps giving me sidelong glances as we walk along a hiking trail through the woods. Eventually, the path winds past the field where the corn maze and pumpkin patch are located. They won't open to the public until the Fall Festival, but I'm eager to see how they've decorated the maze entrance. Those are the only Halloween decorations I haven't seen yet.

Missy isn't voicing any complaints about our outing, but her hazel eyes convey a clear message: Why am I being dragged into the woods by this strange man I barely know? Yet her concern seems less about her safety and more about needling me and stifling laughter behind my back.

"This is what my friends and I used to do for fun," I explain, gesturing at the colorful, balding trees. "We'd run around the woods. Of course, that was before everybody had phones and computers." Missy is silent, though I sense she's still amused by me. "Besides," I nudge her with my elbow, "what else have you got to do?"

Today has been cloudy and chilly, so even though it's not even dinner time yet, the sky is already darkening. By the time we reach the maze, it'll be delightfully eerie. Missy's dressed in a green hoodie and jeans today; I made sure she wore socks with her clunky shoes before we set off.

After hiking in silence for a while, I break it again. "Do you have friends?"

Missy tips her head back to give me a quizzical look.

"You know, friends. People you like and do fun things with." She points at me, and I shake my head. "No, we're not friends. First off, we hardly know each other. And second, we probably won't see each other after the festival. Friends usually hang out more than once in a lifetime."

For a second, I worry I've come off too harsh. I'm not rejecting her; I'm just stating the facts. Thankfully, she doesn't seem offended. She appears thoughtful more than anything else. This is just another odd encounter to add to the list. I'm no psychologist, but I thought making friends was something most kids learned in preschool. Isn't it instinctual to form friendships? Something we all understand without needing to be taught? Even those who have no friends grasp the concept, don't they?

"You grew up in this town," she says. "None of your family lives here anymore, but you come back for the festival every year. It's special to you." Missy looks up at me. "Did you bring your daughter here?"

I had managed to forget the first time she mentioned a daughter. Now that she's brought it up a second time, the initial conversation rushes back, feeling like a bucket of ice water has been dumped over my head. My toe catches the back of my heel. To stop myself from falling, I do a little hop-skip and regain my balance. I shake my shoulders to ease the thumping of my heart against my ribs.

"Oh, I see." I smirk. "You're 'proving' that you know me? Let me tell you something, kiddo. Friendship is a two-way street. You might know a few details about me, but what do I know about you?"

Her expression turns serious. "You know what you need to know."

"In other words, nothing."

Missy comes to a sudden halt in the middle of the trail. It happens so fast that I'm three feet ahead of her before I realize she isn't with me anymore. My shoes crunch on a pile of dead leaves as I stop and look back. She's staring straight ahead, focused on something over my shoulder. I turn forward again, confused. Nothing is there except a bend in the path. The only thing she's looking at is more trees.

Her posture is stiff as a statue; she might as well be carved from granite. Any hint of expression on her face falls away. She is blanker than just a minute ago when her face was merely neutral. In this moment, she's the definition of vacant. I wave my hand in front of her face.

"Hey." She doesn't respond. "Hellooo, is anyone home?" Nothing. I follow her gaze and squint into the trees. "What're you lookin' at?"

A cold breeze rushes through the branches, sending leaves flying into the air. It whistles past my neck, making my ears ache. Befuddled, I leave Missy standing there and approach the bend in the trail. Once I round the corner, I know exactly where I am.

We have arrived at the pumpkin patch and the entrance to the corn maze. How did she see it through the trees?

The place looks great, especially with the overcast sky and the fading daylight. Someone planted fake gravestones amid the pumpkins as well as zombie hands emerging from the earth. Skeletons hang from nooses in the big maple tree, their fake bones clicking and clacking together as they're buffeted by the wind. It all looks great, but the centerpiece is at the entrance to the maze: a scarecrow. There is usually a scarecrow, but I don't recognize this one from previous years. This one isn't a straw mannequin wearing a secondhand shirt and a fleece scarf. This year's scarecrow looks … a lot creepier.

Its arms and legs are sewn from a patchwork of thick fabrics. A black overcoat hangs limply from its frame, buttoned up to the neck and swaying whenever the wind blows. The hat atop its head isn't made of straw; it's a dark battered hat that looks like it belongs to some gun-slinging outlaw from the Old West. Brown yarn creates tendrils of stringy hair, which wave about its head freely. The face … it's difficult to see, but it doesn't really have one. It's more thick cloth, kind of like a burlap sack, with black holes cut out where the eyes and mouth should be. It's actually scary, unlike its predecessor, which had a cuter, Wizard of Oz aesthetic.

I only look away from the scarecrow when movement in the corner of my eye draws my attention to the stalks of corn. Something is jostling them. I take a step toward the fence that separates the field from the hiking path. A boy exits the maze. He wears a dark blue sweater with the hood pulled over his head. He looks like he's about twelve years old.

Stepping into the pumpkin patch, the boy hesitates. Then his head turns toward me. I give him a casual wave. The boy doesn't wave back. Instead, he beckons for me to come closer. I can't, though. Not unless I hop the fence.

"Do you need anything?" I yell over the wind.

"You have to follow me," he says. It's a little hard to hear him since he won't raise his head. The boy's chin is tucked, so all I see is the hood of his sweatshirt and the slope of his pale cheekbones. "You have to follow me. I want to show you something."

His words seem like they should have urgency in them, but his voice is so flat. Not like Missy's. Even though she doesn't speak often, her voice doesn't sound robotic. It sounds like the voice of a real person. Listening to this boy insisting that I come with him gives me flashbacks of terrible middle school plays, where the actors don't even try to pretend they aren't spouting scripted words that they barely have memorized.

My throat tightens, trapping the fearful beating of my heart inside my ribs. There's something wrong with this boy.

Damp, splintered wood pokes my skin. Looking down, I find that my hands are clutching the fence, preparing to jump. I don't remember making the decision to hop the fence. In fact, I really want to do the opposite and run away. The boy comes closer.

"Come on, Mister. I'm not going to hurt you."

I pry my fingers off the fence and step back. Abruptly, the boy stops. He lifts his head a fraction of an inch, and I swear that when I see a glimpse of his eyes, they're black. Completely black. Then he ducks his head again and starts to retreat.

"Never mind, Mister. Sorry to bother you."

I watch him, dumbfounded, as the boy darts into the maze again, the hollow eyes of the scarecrow following him. I know it's just the wind, but the pole holding the scarecrow shifts, whipping the scarecrow's hair. The coat and its saggy, cloth skin twist with it as if the scarecrow is attempting to track the boy's path by peering into the entrance of the maze.

Warmth washes over me as my blood thaws. It feels like I have a panicked hummingbird fluttering inside my chest cavity. I grab the fence like before, only this time I'm hanging on in case my legs collapse and not because I'm about to run into the cornfield chasing a boy with black eyes.

What just happened?

Not wanting to turn my back on the cornfield or the scarecrow, I begin to walk backwards. My hands shake as I let go of the fence. My nerves are cracked and fractured. When my back hits something solid, those harried nerves shatter. I whip around, unsure if I'm preparing to fight or flee.

The sight of a green hoodie and dyed black hair has never inspired such relief. I want to wrap Missy up in a big bear hug. I'm so happy to see her. The feeling fades when I see the look on her face. Cold fury simmers in the firm line of her brow. She glowers at the entrance to the corn maze.

How long has she been standing behind me?

"Did you see that?" I ask breathlessly.

Missy grasps the sleeve of my jacket and tugs on it, pushing my arm until I'm turned around. I only glance back once, and for my trouble, I receive a surprisingly strong shove. In that last look, the scarecrow has somehow turned toward me even though the wind hasn't changed direction.

We round the bend in the trail, and the corn maze disappears.

10

Hush, You Squalling Thing

She was the most beautiful little creature I had ever seen. I never thought I would love anyone more than Rebecca, but I was wrong. As soon as the nurse put her in my arms, the center of my world shifted. Her sleepy eyes were squeezed shut, making me wonder what babies dreamed about. I placed my hand on her head, feeling her fuzzy, thin hair. She had that new baby smell. It didn't even cross my mind to feel silly bringing her to my face so I could sniff the crown of her head.

And then she started to wail.

I had no idea what to do with a sobbing newborn. I handed her to Rebecca, and instantly she stopped crying. Okay, I thought with a grudging smile, I see how it is. Right from the start, she had her parents wrapped around her tiny fingers. She knew how to get us to do her bidding. She really used that to her advantage when we visited Birchwood Lake. If I caught her eye when she pushed her lip into a pout, then I was a goner. That was how she wheedled caramel apples and kettle corn out of me, despite her mom's restrictions on sugar.

Those road trips were family vacations at first, just me, Rebecca, and Little Miss Sunshine visiting my parents and enjoying the Fall Festival. Then Rebecca found a new job that paid better but had longer and less flexible hours. After that, it became a daddy-daughter trip to Birchwood Lake. Once my girl started school, I'd let her skip that Friday so we could start our road trip. We would spend the weekend with her grandparents and drive home on Sunday. I always brought her to school late

97

that Monday. It was only once a year, so her mom let it slide.

I haven't told Rebecca this, and I don't plan to, but those vacations were my favorite. When it was just the two of us. She was a mama's girl from the beginning, and I didn't resent that. But it was nice to have her to myself for a weekend.

I'm not telling you this to make you feel guilty. Believe it or not, I'm not upset that you used her memory in your efforts to manipulate me. I'm only reminiscing now that it's not so agonizing to do so.

After she disappeared, thinking about her hurt *me in a way that was difficult to put into words. Before I met you, I had consciously avoided thinking of her for so long. With you around, memories of her began to trickle back in, and they weren't as painful as they used to be. Yes, it was jarring to hear you ask if you reminded me of my daughter. Thinking of her still put an ache in my chest, but it wasn't debilitating.*

I was telling the truth when I said you didn't remind me of anyone. You didn't remind me of my daughter, but there were times when I saw and felt flashes of her while I was with you. There was a warmth—a similar warmth I felt on those daddy-daughter trips. I hate to imagine that the warmth I felt around you was nothing more than an illusion.

***

It's off-putting how different Missy is in the hours following the incident by the corn maze. I've only seen her angry twice: once when that squirrel screeched at us, and the other when that boy came out of the cornstalks. With the squirrel, her anger dissipated within minutes. It's been over five hours since our walk, and Missy's brow is still furrowed.

She sits on her bed and glares at the door of our motel room. Our conversation in the woods was the last time she spoke; not so unusual given the way she guards her words like they're made of gold, but somehow this silence is colder than usual. As inflexible as stone.

I leave the room to take a shower before bed. Working my shirt over my head, I wince, feeling a twinge in my lower back. There's no mirror in here, so all I can do is poke and prod the area to determine if there might be something glaringly wrong. I locate two sensitive spots that feel like bruises. They're on either side of my spine, right where Missy put her hands to shove me. That girl is really strong.

When I exit the bathroom, I find her in the same position: legs crossed, arms resting on her knees, and fists clenched. Her determined gaze hasn't wavered. How have her eyes not burned a hole through the door? Turning on the TV, I pull down the covers on my bed. My eyes flit over to Missy as I move in front of her. Rather than ducking her head or leaning sideways to look around me, she continues staring through my body as if I'm not blocking her line of sight.

"You gonna sleep or sit there all night?"

I can't tell if she hears me. It's like we're in the same room, except we're not. I'm a ghost to her right now. The mattress bounces as I drop onto my bed. I ought to let this go. Didn't I say the other day that I was done trying to understand Missy? If she wants to glower at the door until dawn, then more power to her.

I set the timer on the TV and turn off the light.

* * *

The sky is pitch black, and I'm in my truck but not driving. No one is driving. The truck is parked on the shoulder of a lonely highway, and the driver's seat is empty. I hear a tap on the window across from me. Turning my head, I think I know who I'm going to see, but I'm wrong.

It's not Missy.

The boy from the corn maze peers through the glass. This time, he isn't hiding his face beneath a hood. He stares into the truck through hollow eyes. The boy taps his finger on the window again.

"I need a ride home," he says. His voice is two-toned; it sounds like it's being scraped by a cheese grater. "Can you let me in? I need a ride home."

I don't feel the same entrancement that I did when I nearly jumped the fence. I don't hesitate to reach across the seat and lock the door. The boy's face contorts with rage. He bangs his fist on the glass.

"Let me in!" he screams.

My hands fly to my ears, and I close my eyes. His screams are like ice picks being driven into my ears. I only lower my hands and open my eyes when the banging stops. The boy hasn't gone anywhere. He has his face pressed to the glass, creating fog as he giggles.

"Do you think you're safe in there? Do you know where she's taking you?"

My body jerks, jolting me awake. I'm in the motel room, tangled in the sheets. Fumbling for the lamp, I finally manage to grab hold of the cord and pull, flooding the room with weak yellow light. Missy's bed is empty. I heave a sigh. I really hate waking in the middle of the night to find her gone. The good news is that I'm not dizzy and sick this time.

Getting out of bed, I conduct a thorough search of the main room and the bathroom. She isn't hiding in any cracks or crevices. She actually is gone.

As I exit the bathroom, I pause in front of the mirror over the sinks. Lifting the bottom of my shirt, I turn and crane my neck. Just like I suspected, there are two livid bruises blossoming right above my kidneys.

I let my shirt fall back into place. When I checked in, I got two room keys and have been leaving them on the dresser next to the TV. They're in plain sight where Missy can easily find them. One key is missing.

At least she has a way back into the room, unlike the first time she disappeared from a motel room. My chest is tight, but I can still breathe. She's fine. She's done this before, and she was fine then. Plus, this is Birchwood Lake. I used to stay out all night running around town and through the woods. I may not be the poster boy for well-adjusted adults, but I'm also not dead. She'll be okay.

I tell myself this over and over. It's not that I don't believe it; I honestly think Missy will be fine. However, there's a voice in my head screaming that I'll lose her. I'll lose her again, and logically I know I'm not thinking about Missy anymore. I'm superimposing the likeness of a girl with golden hair and freckles onto a different girl with brown roots and a pale complexion.

I'm wearing a hole in the carpet pacing from the door to the sinks. The only thing that eventually makes me sit on the bed again is a cramp in my left foot. So I sit, my back against the headboard, and turn on the TV. I try to focus on the screen, but my gaze keeps wandering back to the door.

I hear a baby crying. The sound takes me back to the days when my little girl was no bigger than a loaf of bread. Her head was so tiny that her mouth took up half her face. And when she opened that mouth, she could wail. I'd hold her close to my chest, afraid of dropping her, and quietly chant her name: Nora, Nora, Nora.

She looked like a Nora from the moment I first saw her. Rebecca and I decided on a name before she was born—Nora if she was a girl, and Isaac if the baby turned out to be a boy.

She could cry like no other baby. I'm still convinced that I've never heard a baby louder than her. No matter how much I bounced her, sang to her, or softly murmured her name—Nora, Nora, Nora—she never quieted for me. She wanted Mom. Rebecca would rest Nora's little head on her shoulder and pat her back. Only then did my girl stop crying. From her mother's shoulder, she looked at me with those big eyes and smiled.

A baby is crying.

My eyes are misty, and my throat hurts. I get out of bed and go to the window. The curtains are coarse and light in my hand. Drawing them aside, I look into the dark parking lot. In the space next to my truck is a stroller holding a bundle swaddled in a white blanket. The bundle doesn't move, but that must be where the crying is coming from. A sobbing infant is alone out in the cold.

I'm not aware that I've moved until my fingers wrap around the doorknob. There's a baby abandoned in the parking lot. Someone should check on it.

A sharp tug on my shirt grounds me, wiping away the fog clouding my mind. I let go of the doorknob and look down. Dainty, porcelain fingers grip the cotton material just above my hip. Missy stands next to me, giving me a hard stare. When did she get here? I'm about to ask when she drags me over to the window again. She pulls the curtains back.

There is no stroller in the parking lot. The crying has stopped too.

Missy releases me and walks to the door, securing the chain to the wall. Was that a dream? I don't remember falling asleep while waiting for Missy to return. Not to mention that she seems aware of what I saw and heard without any input from me.

It wasn't a dream, I conclude. There really was a baby in the parking lot, and then it vanished.

I turn away from the window when I hear the ceiling fan in the bathroom come to life. Missy is gone from my side, but this time she hasn't gone far. The bathroom door is open and light spills onto the carpet by the sinks. The sense of déjà vu is strong as I approach the bathroom to find her kneeling on the floor with the water running in the shower. The sleeves of her hoodie are rolled up to her elbows while she holds something under the spray.

Slowly, I walk up behind her, waiting to see if she will make me feel dizzy and sick. Missy makes no move to stop me from pushing the shower curtain aside.

She is washing clothes again: her gray sweater, white shirt, and black skirt. The white shirt appears mostly clean, except for flecks of red along the collar. Bloodstains, and not small stains either. It's difficult to tell with the skirt, but the sweater is a light enough shade of gray that I can see crimson from the collar all the way down to the hem.

"You should soak that in the sink," I tell her. Missy lifts her chin. For once, she looks surprised by me rather than the other way around. "In cold water," I add. "That'll make it easier to get the stains out."

If I was talking to anyone else, I would feel the need to explain that I grew up in a house with very vocal women who weren't shy about sharing personal information, especially if that information pertained to something that was bothering them. Just a few days ago, I would have felt the urge to explain myself to Missy, but I'm not the one washing bloody clothes in the shower. If anyone should be explaining their actions, it's her. If Missy isn't going to explain jack squat, then neither will I.

The knobs squeak as she turns the water off. She wrings out the wet clothes before gathering them in her arms. Water drips onto my bare toes when she brushes past me on her way to the sinks. I stand back and watch her follow my suggestion, filling both sinks with cold water and submerging the sweater and the skirt.

I should be freaking out more. Someone has clearly been injured tonight, and it doesn't appear to be Missy. I can't work up the energy to panic, though. I don't know if I'm just tired or if she's doing something to dull my reactions. It doesn't feel like my head is being messed with.

Looking just as tired as I feel, Missy returns to the bathroom. She seems so small when she sits on the lid of the toilet.

"I'm curious," I say from the doorway. "If you're not wearing those clothes anymore, why bother to clean them? It seems easier to just throw them out."

Her shoulders slump forward. With dull eyes, she stares at the wall. Missy reminds me of an insomniac, craving rest even as she is unable to keep her eyes closed.

"Borrowed," she replies.

Frowning, I point to the sinks. "You borrowed those clothes?" She nods. "Well, I hate to break it to you, kiddo, but I don't think they're gonna want them back after this."

Missy curls forward a little more, the bony curve of her shoulders protruding even under the hoodie.

"Why did you stop me from going outside?" I ask.

Her nostrils flare. "It belonged to *him*."

"Him who?"

With one finger, she taps the corner of her eye. The boy from the corn maze. The boy who looked at me with black eyes. I swallow hard.

"Did he come back for the stroller?"

Missy shakes her head. "He won't come back ever. The little one was still hungry."

Goosebumps cover my skin. I remember how close I was to opening the door and going outside. "You stopped me." I don't know why I need to say it again. At first, I'm talking about the crying baby in the stroller, but then I realize it also applies to earlier when I almost jumped the fence and followed the boy. She stopped me then, too.

I have no idea what that boy was, but somehow, I know he wanted to hurt me—or worse. Missy saved my life, and I'm interrogating her now that she has returned, listless and covered in blood.

Untangling my arms, I hesitantly approach. She seems catatonic as I kneel in front of her. Is she going into shock? I take both her hands in one of mine. Her skin is colder than usual. With my other hand, I smooth her hair away from her face. She flinches slightly, allowing me to glimpse the blood on the column of her throat.

Two deep scratches mark the side of her neck. They're only oozing blood, but I can see a large stain around the collar of her hoodie that is a little darker and a little stiffer than the rest of the sweatshirt. Pieces of her hair are stuck to the wound where the blood has dried.

I release her hands and stand. From the shelf above the toilet, I grab a white washcloth. With both sinks occupied, I turn on the shower and stick the cloth under the warm spray. The pipes creak as I turn the water off. Missy isn't watching my movements the way she tends to do. She continues to stare at the wall.

When I kneel in front of her again, I carefully peel away the hairs stuck to her neck. New rivers of blood trickle down her pale skin wherever the hairs break the scabs. Her eyelid twitches; she shows no other sign of pain. Gently, I pull on the sleeve of her hoodie.

"Come on, Missy. Off."

I help her pull the sweatshirt over her head and dump it on the floor. Cupping the uninjured side of her neck, I hold her steady while I use the warm washcloth to dab at the scratches. I try not to tear off any more of the scabs as I wipe the blood away and clean the wounds where they're still open. It's not until the arm holding her starts to feel strained that I notice she's leaning into me. Her head has drooped to rest her jaw against my fingers. Her body lists to the left, relying on my arm to hold her up.

She looks like a child with the weight of the world on her shoulders.

"It's okay to cry."

At the sound of my voice, I feel her twitch. I clear my throat.

"If you *need* to cry, that is. It's kind of like flushing whatever is making you sad out of your system. Sometimes, you feel better after crying."

I don't expect her to listen to me. It doesn't immediately register the way her hazel eyes gloss over and her face crumples. And I'm definitely not expecting it when she falls against my chest. I have to wrap my arms around her to ensure the two of us don't topple to the floor. A wet patch quickly grows on my shoulder. She doesn't make a sound, though I feel every inch of her shaking.

The expression on her face right before she fell into my arms … I recognize it. It's the look of someone who just lost the most precious thing in the world. Pure despair. It's the look of a man who took a swing at a police officer who bore bad news. It's the look someone wears when life has finally crushed them, and they're giving up the fight.

My grip around Missy grows tighter. Before I know what I'm doing, I'm rocking her back and forth, softly chanting her name.

Missy, Missy, Missy.

11

Old Father Long-Legs

There's someone knocking at the door. I used to answer without thinking about who might be on the other side. Now, I have a short list of potential visitors. At the top is Annika. She lives nearby and thinks it's her duty to check on me occasionally. By her definition, "occasionally" means every weekend. It's gotten to the point where I sometimes pretend I'm not home. She means well, and besides Carson, Annika is my best friend. I just can't stand the way she hovers, as if she thinks my mind might suddenly snap.

Next on the list is Ethel Price, my elderly neighbor. She brings me quality coffee beans and a jar of honey from her beehives. Ethel always knocks first, but she knows where I hide my spare key, so she usually lets herself in. The knock is just a formality.

Whoever is there is still knocking. It's not Ethel, then.

Sometimes, the pastor who goes to my gym stops by. I don't attend his church; we just happened to run laps at the track at the same time one evening and started talking. Pastor Kim is a good guy. He doesn't barge in or yell for me to open the door. He's subtler than Ethel or Annika. If I don't answer the door, he'll sit on the front steps and tell me a story through the door. It's always a personal story. Sometimes it's funny, sometimes it's sad, and sometimes it's a pleasant memory. He leaves afterward and never mentions it when we see each other at the gym.

Then there are times when it's none of those people. During those times, I peer out the window and don't recognize the person knocking. I never answer the door if

I don't know who's out there, especially if it's a kid—Halloween is the longest night of the year. I always need to look, though, just to be sure. Because what if it's you? What if you came back and I didn't answer the door? Would I open it for you? If I saw you again, I don't know whether I would remember the good times or see you as you were in those final moments.

I need to go look out the window now. Just to make sure.

***

The days following Missy's breakdown in the bathroom are quiet. We take walks, hang out in the motel room, and I show her how to play arcade games at Alfred's. Thankfully, no more weird stuff occurs—no more tongues and eyeballs hidden in her food, no more teeth in the shower, and no more bloody clothes, at least none that I notice.

The day before the Fall Festival, I hear about a movie night for kids and teenagers being hosted at the Community Center. I overhear a couple of moms talking about a group of volunteers setting up a projector in the gymnasium to screen *Hocus Pocus*. It sounds open to everyone, with free popcorn and apple cider.

I ask Missy if she is interested in going, to which I get a typical silent response.

"I need a yes or a no, kiddo. Otherwise, I'm going and dragging you with me."

Her shoulders bob up and down, which I suppose is the best answer I'm going to get.

We show up at the Community Center twelve minutes before the movie is supposed to start. The gym is in total disarray. Younger kids are chasing each other and bouncing off the walls, their shouts and laughter echoing in the large space. Some teenagers, who look around Missy's age, have found a cart full of basketballs and are shooting hoops. Another guy is zipping around the gym on a skateboard.

Missy grabs my hand and squeezes, making my knuckles pop under the pressure. This isn't the first time she has squeezed my hand, but she's never done it this hard. Maybe we came to an understanding after our conversation over Swedish meatballs. She knows that I know something is up, so she isn't trying so hard to hide it anymore. Wincing, I latch onto her wrist with my other hand and squeeze back, signaling for her to ease up a little. She does, with an apologetic pout.

I scan the room, searching for an activity she can participate in. Shooting hoops is a no; with her strength, she might accidentally break the backboard. She probably shouldn't join in the game of chase with the younger kids either, given the reactions small children have had to her in the past. I'm about to suggest that she come with me when I spot a table toward the back of the gym. It's surrounded by a group of girls, and pieces of brightly colored construction paper litter the floor around it.

I don't know whether Missy is artistic. All I have to judge is her clumsy sketch of an albatross drawn on a McDonald's napkin. However, it seems like the safest activity for her.

"Hey, look." I point to the craft table. "Let's check that out."

As we get closer to the table, I am accosted by the scent of Elmer's Glue. Stickers, colored paper, markers without caps, scissors that cut in cool designs, and glitter are everywhere. I can barely see the tabletop underneath it all. I do not envy whoever has to clean this up later.

I plant Missy in an open space at the table and pat her on the back. She's older than most of the girls in this corner of the gym. Hopefully, no one will take much notice of her if she doesn't talk. Crying kids would put a real damper on the party.

"Why don't you draw me a picture or something?" I suggest. "I'm gonna see if I can find an adult who's in charge."

She casts me a baleful scowl of betrayal, as if I've just thrown her and a bucket of chum into the ocean.

I smirk. "What? They're only kids. Now play nice, Missy. I'll be back in a few minutes."

The raucous clamor of unsupervised playtime gradually fades as I walk away from the open gymnasium doors. The rest of the building is dark and quiet. Only a minimal number of hallway lights are on, I guess so people can find their way to the restrooms. But other places, like the stairwell to the second floor, are veiled in thick shadows. There has to be an adult somewhere. At the very least, someone who knows how to run the projector needs to be in the building.

Most of my memories of the Community Center involve summer day camp from fifth through eighth grade. I've never been in the building after hours. It's eerie how nighttime seems to magnify noises in the empty hallways. The conference rooms and offices I come across are locked up tight. It isn't a large building, so it doesn't take long to do a cursory search and then circle back to the gym. The only place I haven't looked is the second floor—so far, I haven't seen anyone older than Missy.

I notice the light from the kitchen at the end of my loop. The kitchen is right next to the gymnasium. The main door for servers is on the other side of the building, closer to the space where tables and chairs can be set up for events. This is just the side door, narrow and not meant to be very conspicuous. It is propped open, but with all the noise coming from the gym next door, it's hard to hear the adults in the other room. When I come closer, I hear the microwave running and somebody complaining about the pilot light for the oven.

Stepping into the doorway, I see four people. Two older women are pouring warm cider into Styrofoam cups at the counter. A younger guy, who looks like he's in his twenties, is kneeling on the floor with half his body hidden inside the oven. Lastly, running back and forth between the three microwaves, is a woman who looks sort of familiar. They're all so busy that no one has noticed me.

I knock on the open door. One of the older ladies looks up from the counter. "Yes, can we help you?"

Everyone else pauses what they're doing and lifts their eyes to me. I clear my throat.

"Uh, yeah. I was gonna drop off my niece for the movie, but I can't find the person in charge of this thing. It's just a bunch of kids in the gym."

One of the microwaves dings, and the younger woman swears under her breath. "Did Grant go with Jonathan to get the projector?" she asks the man kneeling on the floor. "You told him to stay here, didn't you, Tommy?"

"First of all, Sharron, I'm twenty-five, not twelve. I haven't been Tommy since junior high." Tom grabs the stove to pull himself to his feet. "And second, I thought you wanted Grant to get the projector. He was the one who helped Mr. Jacobs put all that junk back in storage after the Summer Reading Extravaganza."

Sharron takes a steaming bag of popcorn out of the microwave, expertly rips it open, and dumps it in a giant plastic bowl. "So I told Jonathan to get the projector, and you told Grant to get the projector, and now no one is watching the kids. Perfect."

Another microwave dings. A flustered Sharron removes the bag but doesn't empty it into the bowl. She washes her hands in the nearest sink and nudges Tom with her toe, who has sunk back to his knees with a lighter in hand.

"Hey, forget the pilot light for now. It won't be the end of the world if they don't get chocolate-chip cookies." She helps him stand up again. "Let's focus on getting the popcorn ready first, and I'll go keep an eye on things in the gym until the guys get back."

Tom salutes her. "Aye, aye, Captain."

Sharron marches out of the kitchen so swiftly that I barely have time to jump out of her way. She extends her hand to me as we're walking. "Hi, I'm Sharron Durst. Sorry about this. I thought my brother's friend Grant was chaperoning."

"No worries," I assure her. "It didn't look like they'd set anything on fire yet."

Sharron laughs. "Oh, just give them time. Some of those boys could make fire at the bottom of a swimming pool."

"That sounds like me and my friends when we were kids."

Somehow, it seems to have gotten louder in the gym since I left Missy in here. The cart of basketballs has been overturned, leaving a dozen or so balls rolling around the room. Some of the smaller kids are now inside the cart while one rambunctious boy is attempting to climb on top of it. At least relative order appears to be maintained over the craft table.

Sharron cups her hands around her mouth. "Will! Colton! Jesse!" She points at the kids in and on top of the basketball cart. "Get outta there!"

Reluctantly, they do so. Next, she shouts at the teenager flipping his skateboard in the air.

"Hey, Duncan! What've we told you about skating indoors? You're gonna tear up the floor." Sharron puts her fingers in her mouth to whistle at the group shooting hoops. "Guys, let's have a maximum of five basketballs out and put the rest back in the cart." Then to the girls at the craft table, "Ladies, please try to keep the glitter *on* the table. Thank you!"

She heaves a big sigh and then spins on her heels to face me.

"I didn't catch your name."

"Kevin Wolf," I tell her. Sharron's eyebrows shoot up.

"Wolf? Are you Annika's brother?"

I snap my fingers and grin. "So that's how I know you—you were one of Annika's friends. I thought you looked familiar."

Sharron smiles, putting her hands on her hips. "Wow, it's been a while. I don't think I've seen you in twenty years. I'm surprised you recognized me at all."

Honestly, if she hadn't mentioned Annika, I wouldn't have figured it out. She's right, we haven't seen each other since I turned eighteen and left town. If she and Annika are about the same age, then that puts Sharron in her early teens when I left. Certain features of hers haven't changed, though.

"I think it's your nose," I say. "It still looks the same."

She rubs the back of her neck as her smile becomes a little embarrassed. "Well, that's unfortunate."

"It's not a bad nose," I quickly clarify. "Just distinctive."

"It's okay, Wolf." She pats my arm and laughs. "I inherited the family schnoz, and I accepted that a long time ago."

She believes I'm just trying to be nice. I'm not, though. Sharron's nose is long and straight, rounding off at the end, kind of like the picture of "Kilroy Was Here." It's a little beaky, but it fits the rest of her narrow face. It fits her now more than it did when she was a kid. Her nose used to jut out of her face like a dorsal fin. Annika told me that kids at school would hum the *Jaws* theme song whenever Sharron walked by. Kids can be nasty little cretins.

She chuckles. "This might be a weird thing to say after so many years, but when I was younger, I thought you were the coolest person ever."

"I guarantee you were the only one."

"You hung out with your kid sister even though you didn't have to." Sharron grins. "And you let her beat up your best friend."

I smile. "Carson still calls that Annika's lucky shot. It would be more believable if she hadn't given him a second black eye."

Sharron looks at the table of girls and squints. "I didn't know Annika had a daughter—although, that's not really surprising since we haven't talked to each other in ages. Which one is your niece?"

I bite my tongue. If Missy couldn't fool Mr. Jacobs, then she definitely won't fool one of Annika's best childhood friends. My thoughts are racing to come up with a plausible adoption story, when Missy spots me. She drops the marker she was using and clutches a pink piece of paper in her hands. Putting on a pretty smile, Missy jogs over to us.

"This is Missy," I tell Sharron. My hand lands on Missy's shoulder and squeezes.

Play along.

Sharron offers her hand to Missy. "Hi, Missy. I'm Sharron. Your mom and I used to be friends when we were kids." While shaking her hand, a small wrinkle appears between Sharron's eyes. "How old are you?"

I bite my tongue again. If Missy is fifteen, then Annika would have been eighteen when she gave birth, and I'm pretty sure Annika and Sharron still hung out when they were in high school. She'll know that my sister wasn't a teen mom. Is it too late to jump in and claim Missy was adopted?

"I'm eight," says Missy. She gives Sharron a big smile, showing off her teeth. Then she tugs on my sleeve and gives me the pink piece of paper. It's a heart, I realize. Sloppily cut and layered in massive amounts of blue and silver glitter. I have to hold it with both hands, or else I'll dump half the glitter onto the floor.

The crease between Sharron's eyes disappears. "You look just like Annika! Actually," she says to me, "she looks a lot like you too. But you and Annika always looked alike. Could've been twins."

I chuckle nervously. Balancing the glittery heart in one palm, I ruffle Missy's hair with my free hand. "Yep. They're the spitting image of each other." Missy is still smiling innocently and somehow doesn't have a speck of glitter on her. I place my hand between her shoulder blades and say to Sharron, "Give us a minute? I'll be right back."

I nudge Missy toward the craft table. In the time that I've been gone, the other girls have given her a wide berth. They're all crowded at one end of the table, leaving Missy by herself. They don't seem nervous or edgy around her. It's more like they and Missy are two magnets with opposite poles, naturally repelling each other. I'm not even certain that this was a conscious decision on the part of the other girls.

Glitter rains as I set the paper heart on the table. I give Missy a serious look. Her expression is back to being neutral. Leaning on my hands, I feel the crunch of drying glue and glitter under my palms. I lower my voice so only Missy will hear.

"You don't look eight years old, and we for sure don't look anything alike." I raise one eyebrow, waiting for an explanation that I'm unsure I'll receive.

"How do you know everyone else sees me the same way you do?" she counters.

"That's not an answer."

"You didn't ask a question."

"It was implied."

"So was my answer."

Goopy glue squishes under my fingernails when I clench my fists. Before speaking, I take a deep breath. Fine. She wants to be direct? I'll be direct.

"I know this sounds stupid, but humor me. Can you read my mind?"

Missy has never met Annika. All she knows is that I have a sister. I've never said anything about that sister being younger or older than me. Perhaps she sensed my anxiety when Sharron asked for her age, but she couldn't have known I needed her to seem younger. It's almost as if she anticipated Sharron's question, rushing to me with a childish smile and a clumsy, overly glittery paper heart. She might have some Sherlockian answer for how she deduced it all, like when she guessed that I had a daughter, but I'm not buying it.

"No," she finally responds after a long pause. Then she adds, "You think in pictures and voices."

I straighten up, flinching at the slight twinge in my spine. "I have no clue if you're being serious or if that's an attitude."

Unsatisfied, I rejoin Sharron. She's monitoring the gym like a prison guard, arms folded and sensible shoes planted firmly, ready to intervene if chaos erupts—all with the confidence of a seasoned veteran. She must work with kids or volunteer with them often. It strikes me that she might be a mom now, which is strange because six minutes ago, Sharron was Annika's thirteen-year-old friend.

"You don't have to stick around, Wolf." Sharron only takes her eyes off the kids briefly to address me. "I promise this place isn't going to descend into pandemonium again."

Apparently, Missy isn't the only person who can read people. Sharron is half right: I am hesitant to leave, but not for the reason she thinks.

Missy seems okay now, but what if something happens? What if she does something odd again, and people notice? I feel secure in the knowledge that she won't hurt me. That doesn't mean I'm confident she won't hurt anyone else. Her anger at the boy in the cornfield and all the blood on her clothes … There aren't any other parents hovering, though.

"What time does the party end?" I ask Sharron.

"Around 10:30," she replies. "The start time depends on when Jonathan and Grant get here with the projector. The librarian, Mr. Jacobs, used it this summer for part of his reading program and then put it in storage."

"I saw Mr. Jacobs a few days ago. I couldn't believe he still works at the library."

Sharron snorted. "I know, right? I don't think death could force him to retire. His ghost will probably hang around to reorganize the bookshelves."

I'm smiling—a real smile, not one tinged with caution and a hint of fear. Missy has been good company, but there's something relaxing about talking to a person who is decidedly normal. I should tell my sister to get in touch with Sharron again. From our short conversation, she doesn't seem like she has changed a bit.

"Heyo!"

Two young guys tromp into the gym. One of them is lugging an old projector. The other looks a lot like Sharron, family schnoz and all. This must be her brother, which makes the one carrying the projector Grant.

Jonathan Durst. I vaguely recall Sharron having a little brother, but that's literally all I know about him. He's got to be in his twenties now. Either he's visiting for the festival, or he lives in Birchwood Lake on a more permanent basis. It's possible he never left.

"Hey, birdbrains!" Sharron barks. "Who thought it was a good idea to leave these kids by themselves?"

"What're you talkin' about?" says Grant, huffing and puffing under the weight of the projector. "You're here." Readjusting his grip, he looks around. "Where should I put this?"

"I think there's a stand for it somewhere," Jonathan chimes in.

"Just get one of the folding tables from the closet," Sharron instructs them. Jonathan jogs back into the hallway in search of a table. A sheen of sweat makes Grant's forehead shine under the gym lights. I hold out my arms to him.

"You want me to hold that for a minute?"

Smiling gratefully, Grant exhales a gust of air. "Yeah, man. Would ya?"

We do an awkward shuffle so he can pass the projector to me. The weight of it settles in my arms. It isn't too heavy, although I probably have a bit more muscle than Grant, who looks like he's been carrying it for a while.

Grant sags in relief. "You would not believe how hard it was to find this thing. First, Mr. Jacobs wouldn't answer his phone, so we had to get the spare key for the storage unit from Debbie Shore. Then, once we were in, we had to slog through all the holiday decorations. That scarecrow scared the crap out of us, since we thought it was already up by the corn maze."

"There's a different scarecrow by the corn maze this year," I interject, remembering its dark coat and hat, cloth skin, and the holes for eyes raising the hairs on the nape of my neck. "It's a hundred times creepier than the other one."

Our conversation is interrupted by the screech of a table being dragged across the gym floor. Grant runs over to help Jonathan unfold it. As I glance down, Sharron catches my eye. Her mouth is turned up in a grin, but there's a glimmer of discomfort on her face.

"So," she says, "you walked by the corn maze?"

I nod.

"Me too. I asked Mr. Jacobs why he took that scarecrow out of storage instead of the usual one. He explained that it was the scarecrow Birchwood Lake used to display about thirty years ago. Mr. Jacobs found it in a dusty corner, buried under a mountain of fake pumpkins." She laughs softly. "He called it the retro scarecrow. But I agree with you—it's way too scary for the kids."

"Okay!" Grant shouts and waves us over to the table. "Let's get this show on the road!"

* * *

I don't have much to do after leaving Missy at the Community Center. I could go to the Blue Fox or Alfred's, but I'm not in the mood to eat and drink. I could go back to the motel and see what's on TV, though if I do that, I might as well have stayed to watch *Hocus Pocus*.

I leave my truck in the parking lot and aimlessly wander around town. Eventually, I circle back and sit on a swing in the playground across the street from the Community Center. I've only been walking for perhaps twenty minutes, but I feel dead tired. I'm out of patience trying to entertain another person all week long. Most things I do these days, I do alone, including this trip. I doubt Missy would complain if we sat around all day and did nothing; however, it doesn't feel like the right thing to do. Once again, my mom's personality is manifesting in me.

Checking my phone, I see I have some unanswered texts from Carson, Annika, and Rebecca. All three are very subtly making sure that I haven't taken a nosedive off the deep end into a pool of insanity. I can be annoyed by Carson and my sister hovering over me, but I genuinely feel awful that

Rebecca is worried. After all, we went through the same experience together. If she believes that I'm possibly reliving that terrible day, then it has to be front and center in her mind too. She'll never admit it to me, though. She didn't back then, and she won't now. Just like I also refused to lean too heavily on her. In the end, that's what drove us apart.

I wonder what Rebecca would think of Missy. She would be better with her than I am. Rebecca wouldn't get annoyed or lose her patience. She was a natural parent. I was the one who had to be taught, and after being out of practice for so many years, I've lost my touch. My thoughts wander, contemplating what it might have been like to have more children. If my little girl had become a big sister. I see another little head of golden brown hair and then a third head full of chocolate curls to match Rebecca's. They have my freckles and Rebecca's eyes. When they laugh, they sound exactly like their big sister.

The hollowness in my chest manifests physical pain. Swiftly, I stand and swing my arms. How ridiculous is it to get worked up over kids that never existed? And it's all because of Missy; I never used to think about having more kids after...

I get into my truck and tear out of the parking lot. I need to do something mindless until 10:30 when I can pick up Missy and take her back to the motel. The radio crackles to life under my fingertips as I tune the dial until I find a clear station. I'm just going to spend the time driving. With the heat on, it beats walking and letting my face freeze. I'm not sure what station I'm listening to; all I know is that the current song is soft and folksy. A cello and a violin create a solid foundation while the plucky strings of a guitar dance over it. A woman's voice rolls like waves over the instruments. It's a melody anyone could fall asleep to—a lullaby for a restless child.

In this moment, I hate my hometown.

Recently, I haven't been able to remember why I was in such a hurry to leave. It's gradually come back to me, though. This town doesn't allow people to escape from anything. Everything is so contained in Birchwood that all of my problems knew where I lived. The issue isn't even the people—it's the atmosphere. No matter where I go here, it's familiar. Every place in town has intimate knowledge of who I am. Sometimes, that's a good thing. It only takes a day in Birchwood Lake for me to feel right at home again. But as soon as the honeymoon is over, the old darkness I left behind beckons to the new darkness I've acquired. It welcomes my current problems with open arms, compounding the toxicity of this town.

I haven't felt that poisonous feeling in any of my previous visits—not since I was eighteen. So why now? It's not like I'm dangerously depressed. Back when I first started this tradition of attending the Fall Festival by myself, I was way more depressed, yet I didn't feel as though the town was going to bury me alive. The only difference this year is Missy.

She has already proven to be manipulative. Who's to say this black feeling that hollows out my soul isn't her doing as well?

I'm driving in loops and circles by the time 10:30 rolls around. The radio is on, though I'm no longer listening. My knuckles are white on the steering wheel. At least I have enough presence of mind to realize that I'm being irrational. Missy is just a girl. A bizarre girl, but one who's shown to be surprisingly loyal given that we've only known each other for about a week. Whatever is making me angry, it isn't her fault.

More spaces in the lot are filled now than when I dropped Missy off earlier. My jaw is clenched as I enter the building, trying to keep my composure and not look like I'm five seconds from putting my fist through a wall. It's the strangest thing, though. As soon as the noise from the gym and the sounds of chatting parents hit me, the anger dissipates like fog being burned off by a rising sun. The dark cloud that was suffocating me can't enter the building. It reminds me of that moment waiting for Missy in McDonald's when I considered leaving without her and a foreign sense of panic overwhelmed me. The only difference is that these angry emotions are definitely mine. It feels more like someone reached down to the bottom of a lake and dredged them up from where they had lain forgotten.

Stepping into the gymnasium, I see parents helping their children into jackets, collecting snacks and crafts, and then ushering them out the door. Sharron talks quietly to a couple of parents while two teenage boys look at their shoes, radiating guilt and a little bit of anger.

I see Missy. She sits on the floor with her back pressed against the wall, staring straight ahead. I squat in front of her and offer her a smile. "Hey, kiddo. How was the movie?"

Her eyes come into focus. Then her gaze drifts to the left, settling on the two boys whose parents appear less than pleased by their behavior.

"Yeah, I saw that. Did those two get into a fight or something?"

She doesn't answer, just holds her hands out for me to take. As she grasps my hands, I feel something tucked in her palm. Missy pulls her hands away but leaves the balled-up piece of paper with me.

"What's this?"

"A picture for you," she replies. Curious, I unfold it and smooth out the wrinkles.

The picture is drawn on white paper. Frowning, I tilt my head. It's tough to figure out what this is supposed to depict. There's a stick person drawn in purple marker—no, wait. It's not a stick person; it's a scarecrow. So those yellow lines and orange circles must represent the cornfield and the pumpkin patch. The reason it's so difficult to see what she's drawn is because of all the black squiggly lines. The lines are erupting from the scarecrow, and they've spread all over the page.

"What are these?" My voice wavers.

"Spiders," says Missy solemnly. "Lots of spiders."

"Why are there spiders coming out of the scarecrow?"

She says nothing, but like when she silently assured me that she meant me no harm, I get this resolute feeling in my gut. It tells me to ask a different question.

"How did the spiders get inside the scarecrow, Missy?"

Missy glances left then right. No one in the gym is listening to us. Then she leans in. "The books," she whispers. "They crawled out of the books."

12

When the Sky Begins to Roar

I'm awake in the middle of the night. Again. Thanks to you, I have trouble sleeping. It's not always nightmares that keep me awake, though. Every time I close my eyes, I see things that I was never meant to see.

Do you know where I live? It's not the same place I lived when we met. I used to have this dinky apartment on the edge of the city. The neighborhood was artsy, with concerts in the park, affordable theater tickets, and good coffee. It was a healthy place for me after Rebecca and I split.

Now, I live in a single-level house, not counting the basement, in a moderately quiet and very boring neighborhood. It's located somewhere between the suburbs and the countryside. This is the only place where I don't feel like I'm on the verge of losing my mind. I had to find a balance between total isolation and sensory overload. If I'm alone, I start to see things move in the shadows. If I'm surrounded by people, I begin to wonder who's showing their true face and who's wearing a mask. I need to have some people around, but not too many.

Just because I'm not teetering on a knife's edge anymore doesn't mean I'm okay. Like I said, I don't sleep through the night. Maybe this is why I never saw you sleep—because there were too many invisible predators out to get you. Or was it because you could hear all the howling, shrieking, and laughing that fills the air after the sun sets?

* * *

On the day of the festival, an invisible tension covers the town like tangled spiderwebs. I'm glad I'm not alone right now, or I imagine I'd be feeling the same sort of anger that I felt last night. I don't know if anyone else has consciously noticed this tension, but I can tell they feel it on some level. Just like the girls at the Community Center naturally gravitated away from Missy, the people of Birchwood Lake are naturally drawing together, traveling around town in clusters. Any loners will be strangled by the neurotic web slowly encompassing everything.

A small hand slips into mine, banishing the mounting anger and anxiety to the back of my mind. I look down at Missy, who is taking in the sights and smells of the Fall Festival and swinging our linked arms back and forth.

We both started the day to the folk band playing by the beach just down the hill from our motel. By the time I woke up, sporting a headache, Missy was already dressed for the day. Her cheek was pressed to the window, breath fogging the glass. Clearing the sleep out of my throat, I asked, "What's goin' on down there?"

In response, she pushed clothes into my arms and shooed me to the bathroom to change. I barely had time to brush my teeth before she was rushing me out the door.

That's how we wound up here by the lake, swinging our arms and listening to live music. The sun is shining today. Seagulls pester people for food, and crows peck at anything the gulls miss. I think they're following us; the blackbirds seem more interested in watching Missy than they are in fighting the seagulls for dropped morsels. Missy smiles like she did at the rest stop, except this time it has nothing to do with the crows. She's smiling at the music.

The band is set up right outside the library in view of the beach and the lake. Missy's eyes are riveted to the musicians. I enjoy music, but I've never seen it as something wondrous. That's how Missy looks at the band—awed.

The band is good. The singer and the musicians are talented, though I wouldn't say there's anything that really makes them stand out from other folk bands. It doesn't matter to Missy. She looks totally enamored. While she can't take her eyes off the band, I observe her. The way she drinks in the experience, it's like this is the first time she's ever heard music.

Eventually, my stomach growls. I tug on her hand and gently pry her away from the small concert. Although she doesn't put up a real fight, I can tell she is reluctant to leave.

"They're about to take a break soon anyway," I tell her, noting the time. "They'll be back after lunch, so we can listen to them then."

I spot Sharron by the supermarket. She and Jonathan are handing out orange plastic bags with jack-o-lantern faces printed on them. Kids and parents come by to get bags for everyone in their party before moving on to the stores that are passing out Halloween candy. Missy swings my arm again as we approach Sharron. When we reach the front of the line, Missy widens her smile, playing up the little kid act. It might be my imagination, but Sharron seems to perk up at the sight of us.

"Hey, guys! Enjoying the festival so far?"

"Yeah," I say. "We were just listening to the band."

"I'm gonna go over there later once I'm finished with my shift here. I figured I'd listen to some tunes while I eat my caramel apple." Sharron gives Missy a candy bag with a wink. "I like your costume, Missy. You should get lots of candy with that. I haven't seen many other kids dressed up today."

I'm careful to keep my expression pleasant and unsurprised. "What can I say? The kid's really into Halloween." With a gentle push, I prompt Missy to start moving. "Let's go, squirt. Before all the good candy is gone."

She waves to Sharron and then skips down the sidewalk. Sharron's smile is indulgent. When she looks at me, her expression changes. It's still warm and kind, just different.

"I'll see you later, Wolf?"

I have to swallow to clear my throat. "Yeah, see you later."

Feeling slightly out of sorts, I hurry to catch up to Missy. She is accepting a mini Hershey bar from old Mrs. Grady, who still owns and operates the bookstore. Mrs. Grady wears her long silver hair in a braid draped over one shoulder. I see the elderly woman still dresses in jeans and flannel shirts, just as she did every day when I used to live here. She squints at Missy before complimenting her costume.

If it was only Mrs. Grady who pointed it out, I would blame the woman's poor eyesight. She still refuses to wear corrective lenses, just as she did when I was a teenager and her vision was starting to decline. But Sharron mentioned a costume as well, and as far as I know, her eyesight is perfect.

There isn't as much pep in Missy's steps now that Sharron is no longer watching. Her neutral resting face has returned, replacing the childishly happy mask she wore in front of Sharron. I lift my foot higher on my next step and give the back of her leg a little kick. Missy blinks and looks up at me.

"You're not wearing a costume."

A mischievous smirk flits across her lips for a brief second before she innocently shrugs. That shrug says, *Yeah, as far as you know.*

We go from store to store, collecting candy. The funny thing is that no one is discomfited by Missy like people usually are when they meet her. And everyone comments vaguely on her costume. At no point does she appear to be wearing anything other than jeans and her green hoodie.

My stomach gurgles, and I steer Missy toward Alfred's. Once inside the restaurant, I trade her the rest of my change for her candy bag. She busies herself with the pinball machine while I order lunch for us. Well, the food is mostly for me. Lately, Missy hasn't been pretending to eat around me. Whenever and whatever she does eat, she consumes it out of my sight. It occurs to me then that I'm probably going to get stuck with all this candy.

I set a small, deep-dish pizza on an available table. If Missy decides to eat with me since we're in public, she likely won't eat much. I also set a cup of apple juice in front of her empty chair. Apples and other apple-flavored products are the only food and drink she seems to genuinely enjoy. She'll eat, or pretend to eat, anything I put in front of her, but the only items she chooses for herself taste like apples.

Missy abandons the pinball machine as soon as I call her name. After lunch, I take her outside to play some of the fair games. At the beanbag toss, Missy hangs back to see how it's done. Then, of course, she nails it. She beats me at horseshoes and the ring toss. We're making our way to the cotton candy stand where they're also selling caramel apples when Missy grabs my arm to stop me. Her eyes are trained intensely on something. For a second, I fear it's another one of those kids whose eyes are filled with nothing but darkness. However, she doesn't appear fearful or angry. By following her gaze, I see that she is staring at a table where other kids are having their faces painted.

When we played the fair games, I got the impression she was participating for my benefit, but the face painting is something she is obviously interested in. I give her a nudge in that direction.

"Come on, kid. Get in line."

The painters are two teenage girls and a woman who might be their mom. She's not someone I recognize. All three are decent artists. They paint little pictures on cheeks and hands, but they're also doing full face paint for the kids who want it. I see one boy walk away with an orange and black jack-o'-lantern face.

Missy and I get to the front of the line. Pages in sheet protectors are taped to the table displaying some examples for the kids who are more indecisive. The woman motions us over and pats the seat in front of her.

"Hi, there!" She beams at Missy. Hesitantly, Missy sits in the chair. The woman dips her brush in a cup of murky water and wipes the bristles on a paper towel. "Do you have an idea of what you want, dear?"

Missy leans forward to whisper in the woman's ear. She nods when Missy sits back.

"Okay, I think that's doable. Are you trying to scare your dad?" she stage-whispers to Missy and glances up at me like they're conspiring together. Missy nods. Playing along, I roll my eyes and turn my back on the two so I can't see what is being painted on Missy's face.

While I wait, I don't have much to occupy myself except watching other people walk up and down the street. Observing everyone at the festival feels different this year than when I attended alone. By myself, I could imagine that time was ticking backward. I could make myself believe that a little girl with freckles and pigtails would come running to me from around the corner, the playground, or the cotton candy stand. With Missy here, I'm painfully aware that I am thirty-seven, single, and childless. Rather than the relaxing getaway this trip is supposed to be, I feel all sorts of anxiety. Will I lose track of Missy in the crowd? Will people look at us and see that Missy isn't meant to be here? Will she run off and leave me wondering what happened to her?

At this point, I'm looking forward to going home, but I'm trying to make this fun for Missy, so I take a deep breath and push my negative thoughts down to the pit of my stomach. It's because of that damn tension crackling through the air, I think. It weighs on me any time I start to feel disconnected from the people around me.

"All done!"

A glance at my phone tells me that I've been standing here for roughly ten minutes. Turning around, I regard Missy's painted face. She is a canvas of black and white: a white face with black eyes and nose, and black lines painting a smile across her mouth and cheeks, with white teeth completing the skeletal grin.

"Boo," says Missy with a smirk.

I clutch at my heart dramatically. "That is spooktacular. I'm gonna have nightmares, kid."

Missy jumps up from the chair. I thank the woman and then jog after her to catch up. Wearing a painted skull, Missy's visage is actually less disquieting than that blank stare I am sometimes subjected to.

"Oh, look." I grin down at her. "Now you have a real costume."

Missy gives me the side-eye. If my little girl were in her place, she would have stuck her tongue out. Instead, Missy replies, "Everyone likes a familiar mask."

She doesn't seem as pleased as she was moments ago. The grin slides off my face, and a silent understanding wells up inside me. Missy and I might be on more honest terms now, but she still pretends in front of me to an extent. The reason her blank expression is so unnerving is because she is so convincing when she does put nuance into her features. It's easy to forget how inhuman she can be until she drops the act. Everyone likes a familiar mask. Including me, apparently.

Just like in my nightmares, I have trouble turning my gaze back to her once I look away. A feeling of dread washes over me, one that tells me her blank eyes will pierce me if I turn my head in her direction. Or perhaps I'll see the shadow that drives my truck rather than Missy. I attempt not to look shaken when I pay for two caramel apples. Then I have no choice but to look at Missy so I can give her one of the apples. Blood pounds in my ears. She's only a teenage girl in face paint, returning my apprehensive look with one of assurance. Immediately, my fear settles, replaced by warm relief. A familiar mask indeed.

Soft skin brushes mine as Missy takes the white stick from my fingers. She sniffs the caramel. "It's sweet," I explain. "It's an apple covered in candy. You'll love it."

She touches the caramel coating with the tip of her tongue before deciding whether to eat it. Then Missy opens her mouth wide and sinks her teeth into the sticky confection.

A shiver runs down my spine. I've never seen her open her mouth that wide. It reminds me of a snake unhinging its jaw. There's a crack when her teeth pop through the skin of the apple, and then she tears away the flesh of the fruit. The crunching is loud, and her jaw works tirelessly to soften the caramel.

"Hmm," she murmurs. Missy goes a bit cross-eyed to study the apple held so closely to her face. Then she decides to take another bite, smaller this time. A bite that doesn't raise the hair on my arms. In this instance, it's easy to swap Missy's face for Nora's. She loved caramel apples too.

I swipe my thumb over the tattoo on my wrist.

"I'm not an idiot," I say to Missy as we walk. She doesn't reply, and I wonder if she's as confused as I am. Why am I bringing this up? Regardless, I continue. "I know I'm not gonna find her here. Just like I knew that it didn't matter if Rebecca and I kept our old house. I used to believe that the worst news I could possibly get was the news that she was found dead."

An invisible bubble surrounds Missy and me. Others give us more space than we need to stroll down the sidewalk, as if Missy has activated a privacy mode, repelling everyone so they can't eavesdrop.

"I thought I was gonna get that news when an officer came by our house," I go on. "That's when I found out I was wrong. That isn't the worst news I could hear. The worst news I could hear was that the kid's body they discovered was someone else's little girl. He was taking closure that should have been ours and giving it to another family. That was also the day that I was almost arrested for assaulting a cop." A faint smile touches my lips. "But lucky for me, the guy was pretty understanding."

Her features are solemn but not empty. The intangible perimeter around us widens until the road we walk is deserted except for the two of us—and the crows. The birds land on the sidewalk and streetlights where they can watch us. Their beady eyes make my skin prickle and itch.

"The house was in Rebecca's name, and she sold it two and a half years after we lost … So, the Fall Festival is the only thing I have left. I'm not an idiot," I repeat. "If my girl is alive, she isn't going to show up here. But hope is a hard beast to kill. The worst thing is not knowing, because the unknown will give you just enough hope to kill you slowly."

I haven't talked about this, not since it happened. That's part of the reason Rebecca and I parted ways. The words are flowing now like someone punched a hole in a water balloon. Missy doesn't look at me any differently than she did this morning. There's no pity, no misplaced caution.

"You don't remind me of my daughter," I say with a sad smile. "But I bet you tried your damnedest to do just that. Listen, Missy. You don't have to manipulate me anymore. Wherever you're going, I'll take you there. No police, no questions. I promise."

She looks contemplative, and I can't tell if it's a mask for my benefit or if my offer resonates with her. Missy stops in the middle of the street, her half-eaten caramel apple in hand, while crows flit about, watching her intently; not a seagull in sight. Her brows knit, forming creases in her pale, porcelain skin.

"You're a tree," she says. "With roots."

I fold my arms, suppressing a sigh. Here we go again. "Yeah, roots."

She grips the stick with both hands, studying the apple's browning flesh. "And if the ground is poisoned, the tree gets sick."

"Yes, that's right." I'm unsure where this metaphor-turned-analogy is leading.

Missy lifts her eyes, their intensity weighing heavily on me. "The ground is poisoned," she asserts. "Can you feel it?"

I almost seek clarification when understanding dawns on me. The pervasive tension in town. Something is spreading, and tension is how we're sensing it. Why is she telling me this? I offered to take her anywhere, no questions asked. If something bad is happening, then all she has to do is accept my offer, and she can be out of town within the hour. Yet here she is, warning me cryptically. I don't grasp the meaning, but she's trying.

Frustration tempers the intensity of her expression. "Spiders hatch in hundreds," she continues, "and they're all hungry."

I stoop down so we're on the same level. Her frustration is unexpected for a teenager, more childlike in its inability to articulate. There's another way she can communicate effectively, one she's already demonstrated, without words.

"Can you show me? Like you did a second ago?"

Missy shakes her head. "You can forgive me for scaring you, but you'll never trust me again if I disturb you."

A cool drop of rain splashes my cheek, followed by another on my forehead. Clouds have rolled in, deciding to unleash a downpour on us.

"I don't need you anymore." Missy's face turns skyward. "You should leave, Wolf."

Hearing my name from her mouth sends a jolt through me. During our road trip, this is the first time she has said it. I snort. "Did you ever need me?"

Missy nods seriously. I know I said I would take her wherever with no questions asked, but now that she tells me to leave, I'm hesitant. Can I really abandon her here in Birchwood Lake? I've convinced myself she'll be fine on her own, but now doubts creep in.

"Wolf!"

Another voice calls my name and breaks our silent bubble. Crows take to the air, rising around us in a flurry of black feathers and disgruntled caws. Missy's head snaps to look over her shoulder, her sudden movement jarring me. It feels like realizing I'm nose-to-nose with a mountain lion when I thought I was petting a house cat. The world surges in, enveloping us in a wave of sound and rain.

In an instant, the sky darkens, the rain intensifies, and the clouds thicken. I stand up as Carson jogs toward me.

"What gives, man? I've been trying to reach you for the last three hours."

"What're you talking about?"

I dig my phone out of my pocket, expecting to see no new notifications. But Carson is right. I have four voice messages, seven missed calls, and six unanswered texts, even though my phone hasn't buzzed at me all afternoon. Each message is timestamped for a time that hasn't happened yet, the latest at 4:13 p.m. I check the current time. My phone reads 5:36 p.m.

"That's impossible," I mumble. "We just had lunch."

Carson puts a hand on my shoulder. "You okay?"

"Yeah." I stuff my phone back in my pocket. "Wait, what are you doing here?"

"Well, that's what I was calling you about, but you weren't picking up. The local officers couldn't find you, so I had to drive here in case you did something stupid." Carson takes out his phone and passes it to me. "That girl you said you picked up on the side of the highway. Is this her?"

Displayed on the screen is a photo of a girl, a selfie enhanced with a filter that gives her eyes an anime-like appearance. Her hair and roots are clearly the same dark color, and it's shiny and straight. She is smiling in the picture. The filter is throwing me off, though, and I just can't say for sure if it's Missy.

"She looks like the right age," I say, "but it's hard to tell. Got any other pictures?"

Carson shakes his head. "All the recent pictures are a lot like this one. Her name is Marceline Fernandez. She's from Princeton, and she ran away from school two weeks ago. Her parents were trying to procure this year's school picture for us, but they've run into some issues. They sent us a family photo so we could see her without a filter, but it's five years out of date."

He locates the picture on his phone to show me. As soon as I see it, I understand the problem. Five years can make a significant difference, especially through the stages of prepubescence and puberty. The girl in the family photo appears to be about ten or eleven, with wavy black hair and a round face. Her mother has fairer skin and lighter hair, but the father appears Hispanic, suggesting the black hair is likely natural—this counts against Missy.

Thinking of her, I look to my side. She's gone, as I had expected once Carson arrived on the scene.

"And get this!" Carson's eyes light up. "Marceline went to a private school called Harmony Academy. Their uniform matches your description almost exactly."

"I take it you've got the Birchwood cops looking for this girl," I say to him.

"I told them to keep an eye out, but I didn't want to alarm you or her. Mostly, I had them searching for you when you stopped answering my calls." Carson frowns. "Where did you disappear to? I mean, it's not like Birchwood Lake is a big place. Chief Rogers said he couldn't find you anywhere. I drove like a madman to get here, thinking you might have finally lost it."

Thinking quickly, I explain, "I've been searching for Missy—Marceline. She wandered off a while ago, and I haven't seen her since."

It baffles me how serious Carson can look even with tattoo sleeves and a mullet. He has his cop face on, scanning the area with me.

"Okay. I doubt she'd be able to hitch a ride here in town, what with the festival in full swing." Carson wipes rainwater out of his eyes. "Maybe she went to find shelter from the rain? Or she might be headed for a busier road to find another ride. What do you think, Wolf? You're the one who's been traveling with her."

That's the problem. I'm the one with the best guess, and I have no clue what her next move is. I mentally review all the places in Birchwood Lake that she knows. There's the motel, Alfred's, the Community Center, the beach, and the library. She could have gone back to hear the band play again. Then I remember the picture she drew of the scarecrow. She was going on and on about spiders...

"The apple orchard," I tell Carson. "With the corn maze and pumpkins. That's the only place I haven't checked."

"Right." He leads the way, pushing through the people flooding the street. "Let's do a sweep of the corn maze."

13

He Scratched out Both His Eyes

We're all afraid of being in the dark and wondering if we're alone. You told me that I wasn't afraid of snakes—what I think you meant is that I'm afraid of the snake's unpredictability and my powerlessness to control it. Similarly, you might say that no one is afraid of heights or small spaces. They're afraid of losing control of their bodies, of their fates.

No one is afraid of the dark as long as they know for a fact that they are alone, but as soon as doubt is introduced, they're afraid. No one is afraid of the dark as long as they know there are other people with them, but at the first hint that something foreign is hiding in their ranks, people are shaken. It's a different fear than being startled. Any sign that makes us doubt our control, that shows us the unknown still exists in our world, is disturbing.

You were right on another count. Humans easily bounce back from feeling fear. We can come this close to spinning out on an icy road and then continue driving as soon as the car slides to a halt, like it was no big deal. But ask anyone who's had a genuine encounter with something they can't logically explain, and you'll see that the experience stays with them even decades later.

There were a few times that you scared me, and I forgave you. You disturbed me only once, in the pumpkin patch under the empty eyes of the scarecrow. If I ever see you again, I won't look at you the same way.

You disturbed my comfortable, familiar world, and I haven't been able to set it right since.

* * *

I hear laughter and shouts in the apple orchard before it's in sight. Carson and I take the main road up the hill rather than following the hiking trail that Missy and I walked a few days ago. In the parking lot, I see rows of apple trees. We pass them and the hayride in favor of the cornfield and the pumpkin patch.

Carson's eyes rove over the kids in line for the hayride and those who have just returned, jumping off the wagon. I already know that none of them are Missy. He flags down one of the volunteers and signals for me to wait.

"Hang on a second, Wolf. I'm gonna let this guy know about the situation." As an afterthought, he adds, "I should call Rogers, too."

Watching my friend jog over to the volunteer, my mind races. If Missy is here, she isn't going to stick around for Carson to apprehend her. She has demonstrated that twice now. However, if I come to her alone, she may decide to hear me out. I have to make a decision fast before Carson finishes informing the man in the orange vest about Marceline Fernandez.

I take off at a sprint, running for the path that leads to the cornfield. In a moment, I'm obscured by trees, but I don't stop to catch my breath. Once Carson realizes I'm gone, it won't take him long to assume I went this way. Right now, he could easily catch up. I race around families huddled beneath umbrellas and don't slow my pace until I see the corn maze.

There's the scarecrow, guarding the entrance and lording over the pumpkin patch. People enter the maze, and a few linger to examine the pumpkins, but none of them are Missy.

Behind me, I hear Carson call my name.

"Good evening, Mr. Wolf."

Standing under the tent where people can pay for their pumpkins is Mr. Jacobs. Another man and a woman—I think I recognize her as one of the ladies who poured cider at the kids' movie night—are manning the safe boxes where they keep the cash. The big man smiles genially and beckons me to move under the tent with him.

Ducking out of the rain, I realize that I'm shivering. My teeth clack together loudly. Mr. Jacobs scoots around the other side of the table, narrowly missing the corner of it with his protruding midsection. Even though he is in an area with plenty of space to move freely, he still skirts corners as if navigating the cramped library. He grabs a towel from another table.

"These are here to wipe the mud off the pumpkins," he says, voice booming. "I brought new ones with me, but no one has purchased a pumpkin since my shift started, so they're still fresh as daisies."

"Thanks."

Gratefully, I accept the towel. It doesn't do much for my wet clothes, but I can at least dry my face and hands.

"Do you think your niece would be interested in a pumpkin?" The librarian leans in and whispers, "Don't tell anyone else, but I'll give you a discount as an old friend."

Mr. Jacobs has never looked more like Santa Claus with his white hair and rosy cheeks as he gives me a conspiratorial wink.

"Actually, I've lost track of her." I peer around him to make sure she hasn't emerged from the maze since I took shelter. "You haven't seen her, have you, Mr. Jacobs?"

The man's countenance immediately sobers. He scratches his beard and scans the thinning crowd. "No, I haven't. But I only arrived here ten minutes ago. It's possible she entered the corn maze before then."

He goes to the other two volunteers and asks if they've seen Missy. They both say they don't recall seeing anyone of her description, but it's possible they missed her.

"Tell you what," Mr. Jacobs says to me, "we don't have much traffic in the pumpkin patch at the moment. How about I procure a map of the corn maze, and the two of us give it a thorough search?"

Considering Missy's reaction to Mr. Jacobs when she met him in the library, she is just as likely to run from him as she is from Carson. But I could really use that map, and it would seem strange to turn down help. So, with help accepted and a map in Mr. Jacobs' hand, the two of us enter the corn maze.

Wet cornstalks have a peculiar smell. Without the rain, they would have had a light, earthy scent. Waterlogged, the cornstalks smell heavier, more like mud and ozone. Trampled stalks make the path bumpy, like troublesome tree roots waiting to trip the unwary. Not five steps into the maze, I catch the tip of my right shoe on a stalk that isn't bent flat. Mr. Jacobs offers me a hand.

"Careful, Mr. Wolf," he advises with a chuckle. "I don't have any more towels."

We pause at a fork in the path and consult the map. It isn't as intricate as some mazes. Some places create corn mazes that turn into detailed pictures from an aerial perspective. They use computer programs that map out exactly where and how to flatten the stalks to make a near-photocopy of a sports team logo, an alien spaceship, or a cartoon character. This maze doesn't have any of that. It's just a good, old-fashioned maze with loops and dead ends, and only one path that brings people to the exit on the other side of the pumpkin patch.

"I suggest we begin our search here." Mr. Jacobs points to the path going left. "That way, we can arc around to the back of the maze and then systematically make our way toward the exit."

"Sounds good to me."

Whatever good the towel did me earlier is completely undone in a matter of minutes. Mr. Jacobs wears a baseball cap, which offers slight protection from the weather, but I'm soaked to the bone. The farther we walk, the more noises from the distant crowd fade away. It reminds me of the silent bubble that descended upon me and Missy. As Mr. Jacobs navigates, the sky grows darker, but at the same time, the rain starts to ease up. Soon, the rain stops entirely, and the only sounds left are the squelch of our shoes in the wet soil and the crunch of trodden cornstalks.

"So," says Mr. Jacobs once it's obvious that no one else is around to hear, "this non-niece of yours. What's her story? As you know, I do love an intriguing tale."

It's a good thing the librarian is heading our expedition, or else he would've seen how the blood drains from my face. I was hoping he would forget about that. No such luck.

"She was hitchhiking," I say, going for partial truths. "She was on her way to Birchwood Lake, so I gave her a lift. Missy's grandparents are in town for the festival, and she was going to stay with them." Okay, a few outright lies peppered in as well. "She asked me not to tell people who she was. I thought maybe there was a dangerous situation at home, and that was why she wanted to keep her identity a secret. Stupid, I know. But at the time, I believed I was helping."

"To err is human," replies Mr. Jacobs. "You can take comfort in the knowledge that you are a well-intentioned human, Mr. Wolf. Though they say that the road to hell is paved with good intentions. However much we strive to do good, the results can be monstrously bad, regardless of our aim."

A crow swoops low, landing on a bent cornstalk. It watches us intently. I stand a little straighter and look around; these birds tend to flock to Missy. Is she nearby? I see the dark inkblots of more crows in the trees and a few circling overhead.

"Have you informed the Birchwood police that the girl is missing?" Mr. Jacobs nimbly sidesteps and hops over fallen stalks that arch into our path.

"Yeah, they know."

I leave out Carson's involvement as well as the incident where I lost time. The hair on the nape of my neck prickles at the whooshing sound of the crow perched on the cornstalk taking flight. It's too quiet. I know Mr. Jacobs said they were in the middle of a lull, but Carson was headed my way when we ventured into the maze. I should hear him shouting for me. After all, he drove all the way here from Sycamore just to make certain that I was all right.

"That's good," Mr. Jacobs replies. "The more eyes looking for her the better."

Does he notice how quiet it is? My skin tingles, hyper-sensitive to everything.

Needing something to do with my nervous energy, I pull cornstalks apart to see if Missy is hiding just off the path. This doesn't accomplish much except to agitate the crows following us through the maze.

The silence becomes heavier, making it even more jarring when a few of the birds suddenly caw. It can't be the weather causing this unnatural quiet; it isn't even raining anymore. "Mr. Jacobs," I start to say, but when I look up,

I'm alone.

Confused, I turn in a full circle. He's gone. One moment, Mr. Jacobs was there, and the next—poof!

Frazzled energy zips through every nerve in my body. I begin to run down the path, my heart thudding like a bass drum in my ears. Somehow, after a left turn and then a right, I stumble through the exit and into the other end of the pumpkin patch. The crows following me land on a muddy swath of land, while the birds in the branches ruffle their feathers and call to each other.

There's no way we were that close to the end of the maze. True, I wasn't the one consulting the map, but we were only in there five or six minutes at most before Mr. Jacobs vanished.

On the other side of the pumpkin patch, I see the white tent where two volunteers should be accepting money for pumpkins. The tent is empty. There's no one browsing through the pumpkins either. My only company is the scarecrow, which should be facing the pumpkin patch. Instead, it's turned sideways, pointed at the exit of the maze. Looking right at me.

Where is everyone?

Crows caw at me as I pick my way through the pumpkin patch, stepping over rocks and vines. "Hello?"

No one answers.

"Missy?"

No response.

"Mr. Jacobs?"

Nothing.

"Carson?"

Not a peep, except from the birds.

I stop in front of the scarecrow. Even though it doesn't have eyes, I get the feeling that it's watching me. Now that I'm closer, I catch a weird smell wafting from it. The odor is dank and musty, as I'd expect since the scarecrow has been locked in a shed for thirty years. There's another odor in the mix, something sour and rotten. It smells organic rather than stale, like the stench that comes from a dead animal.

I hold my arm up to my nose, preferring to smell my damp jacket. "They should've left you in storage," I mutter and give the scarecrow a dirty look.

"Not to worry, Mr. Wolf."

I jump away from the scarecrow. Mr. Jacobs' tall figure looms behind me. The two of us are separated by a misshapen pumpkin and a fake tombstone.

"He will go back into storage after tonight."

His rosy cheeks bunch underneath his eyes as he smiles. My heartbeat slows in the presence of a familiar face.

"Mr. Jacobs." I sigh in relief. "Where is everybody?"

"Looking for the two of us, I imagine."

His smile is the same one I remember from my childhood. It's how the librarian always smiled whenever he told us a riveting story.

"Isn't this a fascinating tale?" he seems to say to himself rather than to me. "Two old friends meet again when everyone else in town suddenly fades into the mist." Mr. Jacobs scratches his beard. "Or, I suppose we could tell the story from Mr. Goodall's perspective. Worried for his friend, he rushes to his side only for said friend to disappear into the ether. Either way, it's an interesting premise."

Frowning, I take a step away from him only to bump into the scarecrow. The relief from moments ago sours. Mr. Jacobs doesn't appear worried about our situation at all. Not even curious. He acts as if he knows exactly what's happening. Not to mention, I purposefully have not uttered a word about Carson's involvement. Seeing the mounting trepidation on my face, the man raises his hands in a reassuring manner.

"Relax, Mr. Wolf. There is no cause for alarm."

A flash of movement streaks out of the cornfield, whips past me, and smashes into Mr. Jacobs. It all happens faster than I can follow. The big man crashes to the ground like a concrete wall struck by a wrecking ball. He hits the mud, smashing a pumpkin under him. Bones crack, and a rattling gasp falls from the librarian's mouth.

I'm frozen in horror as the thing that bowled him over sits on top of his torso and punches a pale hand into his chest. The man's anguished cry is cut short as his attacker punches another hole in his neck.

Seeing blood and hearing a sickening gurgle shocks me out of my paralysis.

Without thinking, I throw myself onto his attacker and knock them to the ground. We roll in the mud, stopping only when the spiny stem of a pumpkin jabs my arm. I look down at the person I've tackled.

Spattered in blood and totally expressionless is Missy. Her hands land on my chest, and she shoves me harder than she's ever pushed me before. I land hard, face down in the mud. Getting the wind knocked out of me is a terrible experience on its own, but gasping in wet dirt makes it ten times worse. When I am finally able to struggle to my feet, Missy is back on top of Mr. Jacobs, who isn't moving anymore.

Tens of crows fly in circles overhead, eagerly waiting for Missy to leave so they can get a free meal.

Shaking, I desperately look around for something I can use as a weapon. By one of the oak trees is a fallen branch. It's undoubtedly sodden, and it's not very large. I don't have anything else at my disposal, though. I hurry to the oak and pick up the branch. Closing my eyes, I try to breathe. There's a good chance she'll kill me, but I can't stand by and do nothing.

Shouting a strangled war cry, I sprint back to Mr. Jacobs' side and swing at Missy's head. I hit her with enough force to knock her sideways, although it causes my weapon to snap in half.

Without Missy in the way, I have a clear view of the hole in the librarian's chest. His ribs are cracked open, and there is not much left of his throat. While I was struggling to catch my breath, Missy took the opportunity to gouge out both his eyes, and he's … I swallow. He is missing his front set of teeth. She was pulling out his teeth.

I don't realize that I'm not breathing until my head starts to swim. My body sways, and my numb fingers drop what's left of the oak branch.

This isn't like the times she returned to the motel in bloody clothes. I never knew the guy who came to hook up with Ginger or the boy with the black eyes. This is Mr. Jacobs. He's been the head librarian here since I was a kid.

"Why?" My voice is so low that I barely recognize it. Slowly, I turn to Missy. Covered in mud and blood, she has pulled herself off the ground and is staring at the body of Mr. Jacobs. "Why would you do this?"

Missy doesn't speak. She doesn't move a muscle or even twitch. I don't consciously tell my legs to march up to her, and I still don't feel in control of my actions as I grab a fistful of her filthy green hoodie.

"Answer me! For once, just answer me! Why did you do this?"

I can't make myself stop shaking her. Like a rag doll, she flops in my grip for about ten seconds before she decides she's had enough. Her hands latch onto my wrists, scratching my albatross tattoo. Her eyes narrow, and she squeezes until I have no choice but to release her. I expect Missy to push me again or punch a hole through my chest like she did to Mr. Jacobs. Instead, her grip on me remains, and one leg shoots out to sweep me off my feet.

I fall to the ground, landing with Missy straddling my stomach. Her dyed hair hangs on either side of her face, framing features that definitely don't belong to Marceline Fernandez.

Suddenly, her mouth snaps open freakishly wide, causing her eyes to bulge. Bloody fingers probe inside her mouth. Then her body tenses as she begins to pull.

I flinch away from her, turning my head to the side and pressing my cheek into the cold mud. With each harsh breath, I'm getting damp earth in my nostrils, but I don't give a damn in the wake of this nightmare. I never thought I would know what it sounds like to hear a person yank out their own tooth. I don't start to struggle beneath her until I feel Missy put something hard, wet, and warm against my lips. Flailing, I try to roll and throw her off me. Missy's knees clamp around my sides with bruising strength as her free hand grasps the base of my neck. Instantly, I lay motionless. Cold sweat coats my skin at the thought that she is about to tear out my throat.

Her fingers, cold and sticky, slide up the column of my neck and curl around my jaw. Then she pinches. Pain shoots through my skull. My teeth feel like they're about to splinter into pieces. The second Missy gets my lips to purse, she wedges her tooth against my mouth and forces it in. The taste of copper bursts on my tongue. I cough in a last-ditch effort to spit it out.

Missy's hand clamps over my mouth and nose. I'm out of options. If I want to breathe, I have to swallow. Once she sees my throat bob, she moves her fingers away from my nose.

Something wet lands on my cheek. Missy's face hovers above mine. Her lips are smeared with and dripping crimson.

Distortion bends my vision. It's worse than the dizziness I woke up to after my evening at the Blue Fox. Missy's face looks like a reflection in a wavy fun house mirror. She pulls her hand away from my mouth and plants them both on my chest. Her voice trickles from her mouth in a breathy whisper.

"If you see what I see … will that make it real?"

Something clicks into place behind my eyes, and the distortion resolves. The pigments coloring the land around me are washed out and dull, except for Missy. Her image has a sharpened focus. At least … I think she's Missy. Whoever this girl is, she has my torso trapped between her thighs, but she doesn't look much like Missy. This girl has all the right parts: two eyes, one nose, a mouth, hair, and ears. But she looks like someone cut her features out of a magazine and pasted them onto her faceless head.

Everyone likes a familiar mask.

Missy removes her hands from me and lifts the mask, allowing me to see her real face.

I have never thought the English language to be inadequate. Not until I see something that I literally have no words to describe. *What are you?* I want to ask, but my tongue sits heavy in my mouth, useless.

Missy drops her mask on the ground and stands up. Then, without a backwards glance, she runs into the woods. I only stare at her for a minute before I have the presence of mind to get to my feet. Rolling to the side, I already feel a little less vulnerable than when I was flat on my back.

I catch sight of Mr. Jacobs.

Like Missy, Mr. Jacobs' body appears to me in stark colors and perfect focus. He looks … different. His limbs are longer and more angular. Six extra, shorter arms stick out of his torso, though these have no hands or fingers. The extra limbs remind me of insect legs. Or spider legs. And his face! It's misshapen. His nose is gone, and his lips are nonexistent. Two large holes where his eyes used to be take up the majority of his face, while his chillingly large mouth takes up the rest. On the ground beside him are the teeth Missy removed. They don't look like human teeth. These are fangs.

Too close. I'm too close to him. Self-preservation screams at me to get the hell away. So that's what I do. I run.

14

14

Bye, Bye Lully Lullay

I run faster than I have in years. That thing that was Mr. Jacobs is dead. I know it can't be chasing me, but then I think about Missy lifting her mask, and I run faster. One minute, the road is clear in front of me—no obstacles. The next, I blink and crash full speed into a solid object.

For the third time tonight, I hit the ground and get the wind knocked out of me. This time, thankfully, I'm on top. Carson breaks my fall. We're both coughing and wheezing, trying to regain the use of our lungs. Once we do, and the cloud of profanity falling from Carson's mouth dispels, he blinks at me in shock.

"Wolf?"

We help each other to our feet. Carson looks like he can't decide whether he wants to hug me or punch me. Now that I have my bearings, I note that the colors around me are back to normal. Nothing appears washed out or too vivid. Even the sky is lighter.

"Why the hell did you take off like that?" Carson demands. "Seriously, I've spent the last ten minutes looking everywhere for you! I was ready to get the Birchwood cops over here."

"Ten minutes?" I'm still panting from both the exertion of running for my life and colliding with my best friend. "I've only been gone for ten minutes?"

"What do you mean, only? Okay, I was willing to take your word for it when you said you were fine over the phone, but now I'm calling your bluff.

What's going on with you?"

Reining in my thoughts that are attempting to run amok, I manage to form a coherent sentence. "Long story. You should definitely get the cops, Carson. There's something in the pumpkin patch."

"What's in the pumpkin patch, Wolf? Is it Marceline Fernandez?"

Shaking my head, I grab his arm and drag him up the road with me. Why am I running back toward the danger? I don't give myself any time to reconsider my actions. I just need someone to believe me.

Huffing and puffing, we come to the pumpkin patch. A handful of people stop to stare at us. People—there are people here again. The volunteers under the white tent are ringing up two pumpkins for a man and a little boy; a group of teens emerge from the corn maze as three more people enter it. There is no body in the pumpkin patch. Looking around, I can't see Mr. Jacobs anywhere, dead or alive.

I ignore Carson's worried pleas for an explanation and rush to the spot where Mr. Jacobs and Missy smashed a pumpkin in their struggle. It isn't there anymore. It hasn't been magically unsmashed or something—it's just gone. Like Mr. Jacobs, there is no sign it was ever here. I lift my eyes to the scarecrow and freeze.

A hole is torn through its chest, with straw stuffing poking out, some fallen on the ground. A matching hole marks the scarecrow's neck. The dark aura it used to possess is diminished. It's still creepy as hell, but it has lost the menace I used to feel radiating from it. Now, the scarecrow is just a dummy stuffed with straw.

What happened here? Where is the body, the blood, and the teeth? I'm trying to breathe normally, and in doing so, my head starts to feel uncomfortably light. "No, no, no," I mutter. "He was just here!"

"Who, Wolf?" Carson grabs my arm to stop me from spinning in circles.

"Mr. Jacobs!" Wiggling out of his grasp, I step in front of a couple doing their best not to gape at the spectacle I'm making. "Did you see a tall, old man around here?"

The man protectively wraps one arm around the woman beside him and shakes his head. "No, sorry." Quickly, they walk away.

Desperate, I reach up and touch my face. Missy dripped blood on me, and I didn't wipe it off. It has to still be there. I scratch at my cheek and mouth, hoping to see dark red flakes under my nails.

"Hey, hey!" Carson wrestles my hands down to my sides. "Stop that!" He shakes me. "You need to pull yourself together enough to tell me what's going on with you!"

I don't know how to make him believe me. All the proof I had has slipped through my fingers. Carson says something about getting me to the nearest hospital and instructing the Birchwood police to widen their search for Marceline. A blackbird lands on the mangled scarecrow and looks down at me. A ringing starts to thrum in my ears as more crows join the first. They land on cornstalks, on pumpkins, on the ground mere feet away.

"Wolf?"

At first, I assume Carson is the one who says my name. But it doesn't take long to realize the voice is too high. I turn around. To my right stands a teenage girl in a black skirt, a gray sweater, and a white undershirt, holding a half-eaten caramel apple. She glances between me and Carson.

I recognize her clothes—now adorned with a yellow crest on her sweater—but the rest of her is unfamiliar. Her black hair isn't dyed, and her skin is bronze. Her eyes are whiskey brown instead of hazel. Even her voice sounds different.

Carson is momentarily speechless. Then he clears his throat. "Are you Marceline Fernandez?"

Shyly, she averts her eyes. "Um, yeah … Did my parents send you?"

After that, Carson takes the two of us back into town. Everything seems to fall into place seamlessly. Marceline explains that she was being bullied at school and ran away, intending to travel north to meet a boy she'd been texting. That plan changed, apparently because of me. I have no clue who this girl is, but she seems to know everything about us—what we've done this past week, our conversations, the people we've met. She conveniently omits the bizarre, unexplainable stuff. However, she never gets anything flat-out wrong.

Chief Rogers assigns a female officer to drive Marceline to a hospital south of Birchwood Lake, where her parents will meet her. Carson hints that I should probably see a doctor as well. I refuse outright. He stands beside me as I watch Marceline follow Officer Diane Edwards toward the station's front door. A police cruiser awaits them in the parking lot.

"That's not the right girl," I remark. Marceline looks at me over her shoulder, and I wonder if she heard me. Then she and Officer Edwards walk out the door, letting it swing shut behind them.

Carson sighs. "Let me get this straight, Wolf. Despite her recognizing you, knowing your name, recounting events from the past week that you didn't dispute, and quoting bits of your conversations that you corroborated, you still think she's not the same girl you've been playing house with."

I shoot him a glare. "Obviously, saying it like that makes me sound crazy."

"Well, there's a good reason for that," he retorts.

"Hand to God, Carson." I raise my right hand. "Marceline Fernandez is not the girl I found on the side of the highway."

Exasperated, Carson rubs his face. "Then where is this mysterious girl, Wolf? And how did Marceline know all that stuff without coaching?"

"I don't know! Just like I don't know what happened to Mr. Jacobs' body."

"Mr. Jacobs isn't dead, man."

"Then where is he, Carson?"

"We haven't been able to locate him yet, but that doesn't mean—"

Carson keeps talking, but I'm done listening. No more mystery girls, no more waking nightmares. I'm going home.

No one follows me when I leave the police station. I roughly shoulder open the front door and brace myself against the autumn wind. I can't remember where I left my truck, but Birchwood Lake isn't a large town. I can walk until I find it.

As I march into the parking lot, a dozen or so crows let out earsplitting caws. A whole company of them scatters at my intrusion. Collectively, the birds leap into the air, their wings flapping furiously to gain altitude. There are so many that a cloud of them forms over the lot before it rises higher. In the flurry of motion, shiny black feathers rain down on me.

I storm across the pavement, feeling pairs upon pairs of beady crow eyes watching my every move.

* * *

Just to prove that I haven't completely lost my ability to function as a normal human being, I set up the fake Christmas tree in my living room. Yeah, I know—I'm one of those people who doesn't buy a real tree. But you know what? I burn an evergreen candle, and you can barely tell the difference. I also hang stockings on one wall, one for me and one for Nora. I have lights strung from the roof and wrapped around my fake tree. And I found the TV channel that plays nothing except a crackling, glowing fireplace.

Initially, I did all this to prove a point to Annika, but now that it's done, I think I like it. With soft Christmas music playing in the background, the events of that one October seem light-years away.

It's snowing. Are you out there somewhere? Did you leave footprints in the snow for someone to discover, or are you hiding any evidence that you exist?

The sky is darkening, though there's still enough light for me to look out the window and see someone standing in my snow-dusted driveway. It's a young girl in a wispy white dress that might be a nightgown. Long brown hair falls down her back as she looks out at the street.

Seeing unidentified people in my yard, especially children, usually puts me on edge. However, I don't feel nervous when I see this girl. Maybe it's the whole Christmas atmosphere. I can't picture you enjoying the winter holidays, but if you're alive somewhere, I hope you are enjoying it. I think ... I think I should go outside. I'll be right back.

After setting down my pen and paper, I slipped into winter boots. On impulse, I grabbed a napkin and one of the gingersnaps Ethel had brought me the other day. Stepping out the front door, the frigid air pinched my face like a hundred invisible needles. Hunching my shoulders against the cold, I trudged down the driveway to where the girl stood.

She wasn't you; that was the first thing I noticed. I couldn't tell if she was aware of my presence; she continued staring at the empty street. There was something peculiar about her eyes. From the side, I couldn't discern their color, obscured as they were by a white film. Thanks to you, I quickly realized the girl was wearing a mask, though it didn't unsettle me like yours did. She reminded me of the angel ornament hanging from my tree.

I couldn't think of anything to say except, "You're wearing a mask." The girl didn't reply, but she smiled—a small, peaceful smile. Moving closer, I offered her the cookie wrapped in the paper napkin. This caught her attention.

Turning to me, she confirmed what I suspected about her eyes—they were either blue or green beneath the veil. She gazed at the cookie for a moment before meeting my eyes. "For me?" she asked softly.

I nodded, and her fingers brushed mine as she took the gingersnap. Despite the cold, her skin felt warm. I thought I heard her say thank you, although her mouth didn't appear to move.

Returning to my house, I felt a warmth and safety that I hadn't experienced in months. Strangely, I found myself more forgiving toward you. Now, here I am by my artificial tree and fabricated fireplace, genuinely wishing you well, wherever you may be.

For now, at least.

Merry Christmas,

Wolf

A Sneak Peek of the Next Book in Missy's Trilogy - Now that I'm Alone

<u>*Missy's Guide to Being Human*</u>

Lesson Number 1: Panic

Hypothetically, let's say someone runs up to you and begs you for help. What should you do? If you ask me (and I know you didn't, okay?), there are two acceptable options.

Option One: Offer to help, but only if you actually can. Nothing's worse than making a false promise.

Option Two: Offer to find someone else who can help.

If you're a weasel, there's a third option: Make an excuse about being in a hurry, so you don't have time to lend a hand. But unless you want the universe to give you a swift kick in the crotch, you shouldn't do this.

You know what you <u>really</u> don't do in this situation? You don't look that panicking person in the eye and then walk away without saying a word! That's not just a dick move, it's a sociopathic move. Unless you want people to think you might pull a knife on them on a public bus (which you don't want if you're trying to blend in), you need to show empathy.

Moral of the story: You don't diffuse panic by opening a shaken can of Coke.

* * *

Today is like any other Monday. I drag myself out of bed at 6:30 a.m., throwing off the blankets which end up in a rumpled heap. I discard my pajamas, tossing them carelessly on the floor, then grope in the darkness of my closet for the first jeans-and-shirt combo I find. Without bothering to switch on the hallway lights, I stumble downstairs and fix myself a bowl of Captain Crunch cereal. As I eat, I absentmindedly scroll through YouTube videos until ten past seven, when Dad rises to wake my older brother and sister. Deanna wakes easily, but Axel is always a challenge.

Leaving my empty cereal bowl on the coffee table, I sink into the couch. I half-watch an album review—it's just background noise, possibly lulling me back to sleep for another thirty minutes before the three of us walk to school. Ellison High School and Middle School are conveniently close; Axel, Deanna, and I walk most of the way together, splitting off as they cut through the high school parking lot while I use the crosswalk.

I can't seem to fall back asleep in my bed. My brain whirls with thoughts of everything I need to do before school, only calming down once I've gotten up and started my routine. Then, and only then, can I steal a few more minutes of shut-eye on the couch. I've barely dozed off when I hear Dad's familiar knock on Deanna's door down the hall—tap, tap, tap. Then I hear the creak of stairs under his weight as he ascends to the second floor to wrestle Axel out of bed.

Around 7:30, I stretch and reluctantly get off the couch. I shuffle into the kitchen to pack my lunch: leftover pepperoni pizza, a banana, Ritz crackers, and a handful of Hershey's Kisses from the candy jar. There's one Coke left in the fridge; I snatch it and stash it in my backpack before anyone else sees. By 7:45, Deanna and Axel are zipping up their winter coats and slipping their arms into backpack straps. I follow suit and head out the door with them.

It's December 7 today. Thanksgiving break feels like a distant memory, and winter break is still far away. It annoys me when people start the end-of-semester countdown so early in December. Seriously, could they make the days drag any more slowly?

Axel and Deanna walk a few feet ahead, chatting quietly—not quite whispering, but too tired to raise their voices. Fragments of their murmurs drift back to me.

"...early," Axel mutters. "Left ahead, I guess."

Deanna hums in agreement.

As we near the two schools, Axel and Deanna turn left without a backward glance. I stand alone by the crosswalk, waiting for the crossing guard and his partner across the street to lift their bright orange flags and stop traffic. A group of middle-schoolers exits a bus and joins me at the crosswalk.

My fingers grow numb as we finally cross to the other side. Dirty slush has seeped into my sock through a hole or crack in my right shoe. I push through the front doors of Ellison Middle School, wiping my shoes on the soaked mats, which only makes my sock feel wetter.

The hallways are packed with students since the first bell hasn't rung yet. Everyone crowds around lockers or huddles by bathroom doors. If I had more time, I might fight my way through the masses to Devin's locker, the only friend whose locker is near mine. Most of my friends gather at Matilda's locker on the west side of the school. I won't see them until second period, when Matilda, Hector, and I have study hall together.

The bell rings just as I hang my coat in my locker and gather my things for first period. Slamming my locker shut, I slip a bit on the tiled floor—it's almost as treacherous as the sidewalks outside, like walking on a giant slip-and-slide all the way to Mr. Pierce's classroom.

This classroom marks the beginning and end of my weekdays this semester. I have homeroom with Mr. Pierce and then seventh-period geometry in this same room. I claim my desk in the second-to-last row by the window, though today the blinds are drawn, revealing nothing but gray skies and dirty snow.

Six classmates have beaten me to class, with more streaming in after me. The second bell rings, marking the cutoff for being considered late—though Mr. Pierce usually overlooks tardiness as long as students arrive before he takes attendance.

Taking the blunt tip of my mechanical pencil, I doodle random designs on the cover of my black notebook. The only marks it leaves are indentations, practically invisible unless I tilt the notebook to catch the light. It's like my own brand of invisible ink. Pressing my pencil tip into the cover, I write potential names for my future band; the latest one is Jukebox. I draw wires and robotic lights around the letters, trying to imagine what the album cover might look like. Under my hand, I feel the indents of other similar drawings, testing out different names, while Mr. Pierce takes roll call. I don't tune in until I hear my own name.

"Riley Hanson."

"Here," I say distractedly. I've circled around to the name Jukebox a few times. It sort of has a retro, arcade-ish vibe. It sounds like a band that people would expect to be funky but with a modern edge.

"Riley Hanson?" Mr. Pierce repeats. We both look up, he from his list of students and me from my doodles.

This time, I raise my hand. "I said I'm here."

Mr. Pierce's gaze finds my desk, but his eyes don't focus on me. Rather, he looks through me.

"Has anyone seen Riley today?"

Sitting up straight, I look around the room, waiting for someone to point out the obvious. That I'm seated in my usual spot. That I answered him twice. Becky, Shane, and Trevor—who all sit near me—look in my direction. But they do the same thing Mr. Pierce did. They look through me, then shrug and turn around. Others are shaking their heads, saying no, they haven't seen me.

"What are you talking about?" I speak up. "You guys, I'm right here."

Mr. Pierce sighs and marks me absent on his list. "I know the flu's been going around lately. I hope he isn't sick."

"I don't have the flu." I raise my voice, but it doesn't make a difference. Next, I stand up and wave my arms in the air. "Hey! Hello! I'm not absent!"

If this is a prank, then they're all super committed to it. Even the most easily distracted people in class—people I've seen get sidetracked by a literal squirrel outside the window—remain perfectly still, not even twitching as they might if they were trying to ignore me but failing. Nobody is acting like this is a joke. There's no suppressed laughter or attempts to avoid eye contact with me. And Mr. Pierce isn't the kind of teacher who plays tricks on his students. He's pretty cool, but he's not that laid-back.

I grab my Introduction to Biology textbook—a thick, hefty tome that probably weighs fifteen pounds—and drop it onto the floor. It lands with a thunderous clap that makes me feel as though I'm wielding Thor's hammer.

Nothing. Not a single person flinches.

I bend down to retrieve the book, feeling at a loss and uncertain about what to do next. Awkwardly, I sit back down at my desk. "Okay, you guys got me," I say, just in case. "Really funny joke. You can stop now."

Mr. Pierce finishes taking attendance and turns to the whiteboard. The marker lid pops as he flicks it off with his thumb. "Here is your journal topic for Monday. Remember that I am collecting your notebooks at the end of the week, so your grade will reflect the amount of effort you put into your entries."

This announcement is met with grumbles.

"Hey," Mr. Pierce interjects. "I know it's only homeroom, and you all think the work is easy and a waste of your time. But by that logic, homeroom should be an easy A. So, how sad would it be to fail this class?"

Honestly, it's the best argument a teacher could make to try to convince us to care about their class. It won't work because he's right—it's just homeroom—but his points are more persuasive than those of teachers who claim homeroom is just as important as any other class. Really, who are they trying to kid?

It's easy to push the bizarre start to the morning out of my mind, since I don't usually talk to anyone in homeroom. I jot down a paragraph in my notebook and then return to doodling. By the time the bell rings for first period, I've managed to put the incident behind me.

However, it doesn't take long to be reminded of it. The same thing happens again in Spanish One. Ms. Gosnell takes attendance, scans the room when she gets to my name as if she didn't hear my response, and then asks the rest of the class if I'm at school today. I have Spanish with Shane from homeroom. He tells Ms. Gosnell that I'm absent.

I go through the same routine: shouting, waving my arms, and even standing on top of my desk at one point. By the end of first period, it's finally sinking in that this might not be the most elaborate prank in Ellison Middle School history. I force myself to take a deep breath. I have study hall with Matilda and Hector next. They'll help me figure out what to do.

I run to the library, skidding to a halt at the door so I can check in with Mr. Harrison. He is the most chill study hall supervisor ever. He doesn't care what we do as long as we're mostly quiet and don't leave the library without a hall pass. Some teachers will pace the floor, looking over our shoulders to make sure we're actually doing school work. Mr. Harrison figures we're old enough not to need micromanaging, and if we waste our time, then it's our own fault.

"Hey, Mr. Harrison. I'm here," I say as I walk past him. Mr. Harrison sits on the edge of the librarian's desk, marking students off his attendance sheet as they enter the room. Usually, he looks over the rims of his glasses, nods to me, and says, "Morning, Riley," before putting a check next to my name. Today, he doesn't look up.

Instead of heading straight to our usual table where Matilda, Hector, and I sit, I linger in front of him.

"Mr. Harrison," I repeat. He looks up, and for a split second, I think he sees me. But his eyes shift left and right before he returns to the papers he's grading while waiting for second period to begin.

I break into a run—something that would get me in trouble if any of the teachers saw. I swing around the H through K aisle. Our table is on the other side, by a window overlooking a hardware store and a McDonald's billboard. Matilda is already here, her plain brown hair a tangled mess hanging around her shoulders. She taps her pen on the table as she stares at a book for honors English class, which we all tried to talk her out of taking. Honors classes don't count for much until high school, but she went for it anyway. Matilda will never admit it was a mistake, but we know from how many pen caps that she has stress-chewed into oblivion.

Matilda looks up and smiles at me. "Hey."

I don't realize how tense I am until it all drains out of me at once. "Hey," I sigh. "Wow, you don't know how relieved I am to hear someone say hi to me today."

Just then, someone clips my shoulder hard, causing me to drop my books. My arm throbs as Hector brushes past me. Matilda's eyes, which I assumed were on me, follow Hector. He sits in the chair opposite her and dumps his

U.S. History textbook on the table. Now I'm pissed; it's all I can do not to throw my books at them after I stoop to retrieve them.

Hector looks around our corner of the library. "Where's Riley?"

The second bell rings in the hallway, signaling the start of second period.

Matilda shrugs. "You beat him here, I guess."

"That's weird." Hector scratches his head and flips his hair to the side. It doesn't stay, falling back into place when he opens his textbook. "He's never late."

"I'm not late," I snap as I throw my things on the table. "I'm right here. You almost dislocated my shoulder a few seconds ago. Does that sound familiar?"

"Yeah," she says. "Devin's usually the one that's late to class. Or he doesn't show up at all."

Hector laughs. "How has Devin not been held back since fifth grade? Seriously. He doesn't go to class, I've never seen him do or turn in homework, and he's always getting C's on tests. Can't you get arrested for truancy?"

"I think you're only truant if you're not actually in the building," Matilda replies. "And technically, Devin doesn't leave campus."

And just like that, my absence is completely dismissed by them. Like everyone else, they assume I stayed home sick. Black spots invade my vision. My friends sound distant, as though they're underwater. I grip the edge of the table, inhaling and exhaling shallowly. In my whole life, I've only fainted once, but I remember exactly what it felt like. So, I know I'm about ten seconds from passing out if I can't get my hyperventilating under control. Lowering my forehead to the table, I close my eyes and start taking deep breaths. Two full minutes go by before I can stand without swaying back and forth.

Matilda and Hector are still talking quietly like I'm not here.

They wouldn't do this to me, not when I was doubled over having a panic attack right in front of them. They would be out of their seats and holding me up, offering to bring me to the nurse's office. This isn't a joke or a prank. This is real.

Abandoning my books at the study table, I reach into my pocket for my phone. With trembling fingers, I scroll through my contacts and tap Mom's number. I lean against the wall, eyes burning, as I listen to the phone ring. It rings and rings and rings. The call never goes through.

I hang up and try a second time with the same result. I call Dad next, and it happens again. I move on to Axel and then Deanna. Then I call Aunt Paula and Great-Uncle Sherman. The phone rings endlessly. I can't even leave them voicemail messages. I start sending out texts to every one of my contacts, praying that someone will respond. My texts generate an error message saying that they failed to be sent. I'm starting to hyperventilate again.

Shoving my phone back into my pocket, I flee from the library. The school office is quiet as I burst in. None of the faculty looks up, unconcerned by the commotion I'm causing. I rush to Mr. Jefferson at the reception desk.

"Can I use the phone, please?" My voice cracks. "I don't feel good, and my phone isn't working. I need to call my mom."

As soon as I duck my head to wipe my nose on my sleeve, the tears behind my eyes feel closer to the surface. Somehow, I'm still surprised when Mr. Jefferson ignores me like everyone else.

I run from the office and head for the nearest exit. The door ejects me into the faculty parking lot. I sprint around the side of the building towards the street dividing the two schools. Traffic is a fleeting concern as I dash across. Never have I been so grateful to live nearby, reaching home in under five minutes. Panting, I retrieve the spare key taped beneath the empty flowerpot by the porch.

Both my parents work during the day, so I know nobody is here. I just couldn't stay at school when everyone is acting like I don't exist.

Once inside, I immediately check the photos on the wall. My school picture is still in its frame, and I haven't vanished from any family pictures either. So, my existence isn't being systematically erased. It doesn't explain why the people at school won't—or can't—acknowledge me. I guess I could've predicted that I still exist, considering my teachers called my name during attendance, and Matilda and Hector briefly wondered where I was. It's just that everyone moved on so fast, as if my absence wasn't a big deal.

Okay, let's approach this more scientifically. If this were an experiment,

I couldn't just observe one test group. I need a control group to compare against. I also need a hypothesis. I think back to earlier this morning. Did any of my family acknowledge me? No, but that's not unusual for a Monday morning.

At the moment, my hypothesis is that, for some reason, everyone who knows me is unable to see or hear me. I'm observing the test group first, which is backwards, but it's where I am. Now, I need to observe the control group: people I've never had contact with ever.

I left my coat at school, so I layer up, adding a zip-up hoodie over my sweater and grabbing a hat, scarf, and gloves from the closet.

It's mid-morning, so most adults are at work and most kids are in school. I'm not sure where to find strangers in public. Maybe I'll try the gas station four blocks away—or Target! There are always people at Target. I can try to get employees and shoppers to notice me.

The closest Target store is slightly farther away than the gas station. As long as I keep a brisk pace, I don't have to worry about freezing. As I walk, I keep a close eye on the few people who pass me on the sidewalk. It's not unusual for strangers to avoid eye contact and ignore each other on a city sidewalk, but now I'm wondering if it's because of social norms or because they just don't see me.

In no time, I arrive at my destination. Warm air washes over me as I walk through the automated doors. The red and white color scheme stands out brightly against the dreary backdrop outside. There's a bustling atmosphere here that would be absent at the gas station. This is where all the stay-at-home parents come to get their shopping done. I approach the first person in a red vest that catches my eye, a guy with red hair who looks old enough to be in college, and tap him on the shoulder.

"Excuse me?"

He looks up when a coworker calls to him and then walks away from me without a word.

Next, I go to the electronics section and ask another employee where I can find the most violent video games they offer. I don't get a response. Not even a raised eyebrow or a suspicious question about whether I should be in school right now.

A woman with a little girl in the seat of her shopping cart walks toward me. She has another kid, a boy who looks like he might be five years old, hanging off the side of the cart. She keeps snapping at him to get down and walk, which he does for a couple of seconds before hopping back onto the cart. Purposefully, I walk into their path, causing the squeaky wheels to hit the side of my shoe. The cart jerks to the right, shaking its contents of groceries.

"Braden!" the woman scolds the boy impatiently. "How many times do I have to tell you not to get your feet so close to the wheels?"

"It wasn't me!" Braden whines.

His mom reaches around the cart and grabs his arm. "Seriously, I have had it up to here!" She drags him alongside her and continues down the aisle pushing the cart one-handed while both kids cry.

In one last attempt to draw attention to myself, I find a round rack of clothes in the women's section. Puffy winter coats on hangers are squished together. I wrap my fingers around the rack and give it a shove. It slides across the carpet a few inches and tilts a little but doesn't fall. Huh. Those racks are heavier than they look. I give it another go, this time really putting my back into it. It catches on an uneven part of the carpet, tips, and then crashes to the ground.

Two women just feet away continue to browse. An employee hurriedly walks by carrying a price scanner. No one even glances my way. It's like, because I was the one who knocked over the rack of coats, no one heard or saw it.

I sprint out of the store and run all the way home.

Google is my next step. I sit at the desk in my bedroom and search for people who have mysteriously vanished. I also look up conditions where people believe they can't be seen, wondering if I might have some kind of neurological disorder. The stories of missing people don't provide answers; instead, they unsettle me. The closest thing I find to a neurological disorder is Cotard's Syndrome, where someone alive believes they're dead.

Ultimately, the internet doesn't give me answers. I crawl into bed after that, pulling the blankets over my head, pressing my face into my pillow. This has been my bedroom since infancy; I've laid my head here almost every night for the past fourteen years. The smell of my pillowcase is the most familiar scent in my whole world. I can't help but feel like it, too, could abandon me at a moment's notice.

Eventually, I fall asleep deeply. My stomach wakes me sometime later, growling loudly. As I uncover my face, I glance at the digital clock near my bed. Startled, I jump to my feet—it's almost three in the afternoon!

I rush downstairs, grabbing a granola bar and shoving my feet into my shoes. Skipping layers, I head around the block back to school. I need to retrieve my stuff and meet Axel and Deanna. Maybe I've been invisible long enough that it's starting to wear off, and my siblings will be able to see me. Even after this morning and my Target run, my brain is still trying to rationalize what's been happening today. Perhaps this is something everyone in my family goes through. I picture Axel saying, "Oh yeah! Six months after I turned fourteen, I was invisible for a day too."

I run down the sidewalk, splashing through slushy puddles, not caring that my socks are getting wet. The crossing guards are just setting up as I dash across the street. I don't stop to wait for them to acknowledge me; I don't need that kind of confirmation while hope still has my spirits soaring. I make it inside the building just as the final bell rings. In seconds, the halls fill up, and I fight through the crowd of students to reach my locker. I think I left some things in the library, but I don't really care about them right now.

Opening my locker, I half expect to find notes from friends stuffed inside, but there are none. Before I can be disappointed, I remind myself that when any of them are absent, I usually wait until the very end of the day to leave a note. I haven't vanished off the face of the planet; I still exist. Odds are, my friends will drop by any minute now to shove a note into my locker.

My backpack straps are snug over my puffy winter coat. It feels odd sliding my arms through them after barely being at school today. By some miracle, I spot Devin coming from the other end of the hallway, fighting his way toward me. His red cowlick stands out among blondes and brunettes. Devin's shorter than most guys our age, usually getting lost in crowds, so spotting him feels like a stroke of luck. I consider yelling his name, but before I decide, he disappears from sight. Hector, Elisa Chen, and Kai Brenner all take the bus, so they'll have to rush to collect their things. No lagging or they'll miss their ride home. I'm pretty sure Devin walks, and Matilda's mom drives her, so they're my only friends who might linger after the bell.

I walk to the entryway, near the doors where I always wait for Axel and Deanna. I keep an eye out for Matilda, even though I know she couldn't see me earlier. I just want some familiar comfort; Matilda is the one in our group who always has answers, or knows how to find them. If I could talk to her somehow, she would know what's happening to me.

Before I catch sight of Matilda, Axel and Deanna walk through the doors. Axel is seventeen, Deanna sixteen, with just over a year separating them. They've always been best friends, which everyone tells me is strange. Since I can remember, they've done everything together—sports, parties, and picking me up from school. Today, they stand off to the side, talking and laughing as they wait for me.

I elbow through students to reach them. "Hey, guys."

Axel smirks. "Oh, come on, Dee. It'll be fun! You can wear your Wonder Woman costume again."

Deanna groans. "That costume was terrible, and you know it."

My hopes rise briefly, but they must have been too high, because they plummet fast. They can't hear me. Their faces are turned toward each other, so I wave my hand between them, but I get no reaction. They can't see me either.

What do I do now? The burning behind my eyes and the tightness in my throat reflexively fight off tears, even though no one will notice. Deanna and I are almost the same height now, but I'm still short enough to easily wrap my arms around her and rest my head on her shoulder. I tuck my forehead into the hollow between her neck and shoulder, where she's ticklish, but she doesn't react. It's been a long time since I ran to my sister for help or reassurance. When I was little, I'd hug Deanna if Axel picked on me.

This time, she doesn't return my hug, continuing to talk to Axel about a movie they plan to see next weekend. I let go when Deanna walks away, jostling me aside. The entryway is mostly empty now. She and Axel venture farther into the building, peering down the long hallway in both directions.

"Where is he?" She sounds annoyed, likely preparing to scold me as soon as I reveal myself. "Seriously, how long have we been waiting? Like, twenty minutes?"

Axel shrugs. "Does Riley have after-school stuff? Isn't he in the band or something?"

Deanna and I roll our eyes. "No, Axel. He wants to start his own band, but he isn't in the school band."

"Well, how am I supposed to know that?" Axel mutters.

"Come on." Deanna grabs his hand. "Let's find one of Riley's teachers and see if they know where he is."

I trail behind them as they visit Mr. Pierce and other teachers Deanna remembers me mentioning. My teachers all tell them the same thing: that I wasn't here today.

Finally, both Deanna and Axel are starting to look worried. They return to the front doors. Deanna is pale and wide-eyed, clutching Axel's sleeve. "Axel, did Riley even make it to school?" I've never heard my sister's voice sound so fragile. Axel frowns and grips Deanna's elbow to steady her. He looks around as if expecting me to pop out from behind the trophy case or the vending machines at any moment.

"Of course he did. He left early and beat us here."

I gape at my brother. "I left early?! When have I ever done that, you idiot?"

"Did he, though?" Deanna insists.

Yes, Dee! Be the voice of reason!

"Riley hasn't left without us in the past," she continues.

"Where else would he have gone?" Axel's hands clench into fists. "His empty cereal bowl was on the coffee table, and his backpack was gone. Unless..." He trails off and then smirks. "Hey, maybe Riley played hooky!"

Incredulously, I stare at Axel. "Have you ever met me?" I ask him. "I get acid reflux when I lie about doing my chores."

Deanna smacks his arm. "Be serious, Axel! In what universe would Riley skip school?"

"He could have. We don't know everything about him."

"So where is he?" she practically shouts.

"I don't know, okay! I don't know."

This is as close to fighting as I've ever seen them get, not including the annual argument over which Christmas ornaments to hang on the tree. Who would've thought they would fight over me? Deanna looks how I must have looked this morning: pale, tearful, breathing shallowly.

"We're dead," she gasps. "When Mom and Dad find out, we're dead." Then she stops pacing and somehow grows paler. "What if Riley is dead?"

Axel lurches forward and grabs her by the shoulders before she can keel over. "Don't jump to conclusions, all right? Riley is fine. I'm sure we'll find him at one of his little friends' houses. Mom has all the parents' phone numbers written in her address book. We'll go home, and we'll call every single one of them if we have to."

Taking deep breaths to match Axel's, Deanna nods.

And this whole argument takes place with me literally standing in the middle of it. Obviously, whatever is making me invisible hasn't worn off.

With nowhere else to go and nothing else to do, I follow my brother and sister outside. In their mounting panic, they soon outpace me. I lag behind, utterly exhausted.

The crossing guards look antsy. They probably only have another ten minutes or so before they can go inside and put away their vests and flags. There are still a handful of kids waiting to be picked up, standing in the carpool area behind a waist-high fence. Two of them see their rides pull up to the curb, and they rush down the sidewalk. For the second time today, my shoulder gets clipped, and this time, my foot slips on a patch of ice. I land hard on my tailbone, feeling bruised, cold, and wet.

Wincing, I curl in on myself until the two kids that knocked me over have gone. I sit up slowly, but I don't notice the third person walking toward me until it's too late to dive out of the way. Seeing movement in the corner of my eye, I cover my head with my arms and brace myself. I used to believe being invisible would be a cool superpower. Now, I'm just counting the number of times I've been bumped into and stepped on in eight hours.

The footsteps stop in front of me. Hesitantly, I raise my head and see a pair of feet. Sock-covered feet. No shoes. My eyes travel up the person's jean-clad legs, taking in the sight of a dark green hoodie with no jacket or coat. It's a girl, I note. Caramel-colored curls hang around her shoulders. Her chin is tipped down. Mutely, I stare at the girl.

She's the first person all day to look directly at me. Not past me, not through me. At me. I clear my throat.

"Can you see me?"

Rather than answer, the girl abruptly bends over and grabs my wrists. With strength that contradicts her stature, she yanks me to my feet. And then, without a word or another glance, she walks away.

Read more in the sequel to My Dark Passenger: Now that I'm Alone.

About the Author

Traumatized as a child by the haunted house at the Minnesota State Fair, McKenzie Rae decided to take that fear and use it to write as many twisted, spooky, and mysterious tales as she could think of. As a result, she is still afraid of the dark, and some nights, she is convinced that a monster is under her bed. But that could just be her cat.

Rae prefers to create fantasy worlds where anything can happen. *The Dysfunctional Trilogy* were the first three books she ever published. Since then, she has gone on to write even more chilling tales.

With every book she writes, Rae brings the dark worlds in her imagination to life, and she invites all of you to explore them with her.

You can connect with me on:
- https://www.authormckenzierae.com
- https://www.instagram.com/kenzi707rae
- https://www.goodreads.com/author/show/17380566.McKenzie_Rae
- https://www.bookbub.com/profile/mckenzie-rae

Subscribe to my newsletter:
- https://forms.wix.com/092e2b78-3362-49b2-96a1-47fbf43066a8:a73fbcac-fcc0-4839-ba04-5c105d073da1